The Faberge Easter Egg and Murder

A Parker Bell Cozy Mystery (Book 3)

Sharon E. Buck

Although this is a work of fiction and a figment of my imagination, the characters Anne and Chauncey Livingstone are based on very dear friends of mine. Of course, I have their permission to use them as characters. All of the information regarding the history behind the Fabergé eggs is true as is the Russian nobility dynamics.

CONTENTS

DEDICATION

To Anne and Chauncey Bancroft, the true Tsar and Tsarina

CHAPTER 1

"You'll never guess what I heard!" The voice on the other end of my cell phone was breathless, giddy, surprised, and quite delighted. I was immediately suspicious and immediately started to set up emotional barriers to protect myself from what I knew was coming.

"Gracie Blanche, take a deep breath and slow down." Much as I was already mentally starting to kick myself, I couldn't help it and asked, "What did you hear?"

My stomach tensed, my body stiffened, and I could feel a headache coming on. The good news was I had just poured a cup of Wake-Up Call coffee, my latest coffee-of-the-month club selection.

Holy Moly, that stuff was strong! I poured a wee bit in the sink under the guise of "saving some for Jesus." I added some hot tap water to my cup to dilute it a little so my eyes could refocus and I didn't look like a meth addict.

"I heard that Anne and Chauncey might have a Fabergé egg they will display at the Full Moon Spring Solstice Antique Show. Oh, think how glorious that will be! We'll have national news coverage and more people will come to our town to see how wonderful it is here."

An unsolicited groan slipped through my mouth and over my lips before I could stop it.

Gracie Blanche barely noticed it since she was blathering on about another full moon antique show. Po'thole, technically pronounced Poat, like goat, Hole, was called Po Ho by the natives and Pothole by anyone north of the Georgia state line, had more full moon antique shows and festivals than there were moons during a normal calendar year. Rarely did the antique shows ever fall on an actual full moon.

I guess the original organizers thought it might be fun to thumb their noses at the suckers who would attend a full moon show even when the moon was only a quarter full. Of course, they might have been imbibing some donkey punch at the same time they were setting up the schedule for the various festivals.

Silently berating myself for the uncontrollable thoughts that were already sliding through my mouth, I said, "Why would Anne and Chauncey bring a Fabergé egg to a no-nothing antique show in Po'thole when they could go to a much larger city and show it off there? That doesn't make any sense."

A snort, a deep inhaling of air was coming from the other end of the phone. Gracie Blanche is my oldest friend since fourth grade and our love-hate relationship has been going on for years. We have each other's backs on important issues but we also vie to see how much we can annoy the other one without severing our friendship. This was one of those times where I could yank her chain a little.

I recognized the sounds of her deep breathing techniques to calm herself. She had learned these from Yogi Parmesana when he blew into town a number of years ago. She thought he was the greatest thing since sliced bread. He thought the same thing.

The River County Sheriff's Department didn't think so since they arrested him on fraud charges and escorted him out of town several days later...into the FBI's loving arms. Turns out he was flim-flamming people across state lines and the FBI takes a rather dim view of that type of entrepreneurial spirit.

Yogi Parmesana, real name Albert Thomas, is now residing at a permanent government-funded state resort for the next four years or so. He can continue his meditation practices to his heart's content. Although rumor has it he's not happy there.

Who recognized the yogi for the fraud that he was and turned him in? I would have guessed it was someone from the largest Baptist church in town, but it turns out that it was Mary Jane of the infamous Lady Gatorettes.

Turns out that Mary Jane had taken yoga classes when she lived in Atlanta and she knew there wasn't a yoga pose called swimming turtle or resting crab. But she had him for sure on the snapping gator pose. He did the Gator Chomp in class.

As a founding member of the Lady Gatorettes, Mary Jane lived, breathed, and embodied everything having to do with the University of Florida Gator football team. She was past being an ardent fan, she was a rabid, fanatical fan.

Doing the Gator Chomp and trying to pass it off as a snapping gator yoga pose was the kiss of death for Yogi Parmesana. He was lucky she hadn't killed him right there in front of the other half dozen women twisting their bodies around in unnatural positions wearing their fashionable stretchy yoga pants with matching headbands.

I later surmised the only reason why she hadn't was because she could definitely be identified as the murderer and I knew for a fact she didn't want to spend any time incarcerated at the new River County jail facility.

Mary Jane had actually called me wanting to know who I knew at the FBI so she could report this travesty and have this menace removed from society. Yes, I gave her the names of several FBI folks who could help her with this. And, no, Gracie Blanche does not need to know I was ever involved in this. Some things are just better left unsaid. Plus, I value my life.

Let me back up here a moment and introduce myself. I am Parker Bell, owner of a computer security consulting firm and national bestselling crime author. After escaping from the confines of a rural, economically depressed, and limited thinking little town located on the beautiful St. Johns River in Northeast Florida to the large metropolis of Atlanta, I created a very successful computer security consulting company. Believing that both sides of my brain needed to be balanced, I started writing true crime novels. No one was more surprised than I was when my books became New York Times bestsellers.

I'm in my mid-thirties…or maybe a year or two older…I'm not particularly vain about my looks, although I do have my moments. I'm the height of your average female, five foot four inches to those of you not in the know. I can be somewhat sarcastic at times. Okay, most of the time, but I do try, sorta, to keep my mouth under control. Sigh, it's pretty much a losing battle.

I have baby fine brown hair that refuses to conform to any type of beauty treatment, better known as I gave up on trying to do anything with it, and it's straight as a board…unless I don't run a comb through it after a shower and then it looks like I've stuck my finger in an electrical outlet. Oh, yeah, I have brown eyes.

My exercise routine consists of bending my elbow numerous times throughout the day with my very large coffee mug and doing senior exercises with Deron at GrowYoungFitness.com. Hey, I'm lazy and he has great exercises I can do while sitting in my chair.

While I tolerate my photo on the back cover of my books, I would prefer never to see my picture on the FBI's most wanted list. I don't take a good picture and the FBI is not known for their aesthetically creative posing skills.

I try hard not to go back to Po'thole. I didn't like it when I grew up there, I sure didn't miss it for the some twenty years I managed to stay away, and I sure as heck didn't much care for it the two times when I went back last year.

Inquiring minds are asking why on God's green earth did I ever go back to Po'thole when I disliked it so intensely? Well, the answer is that tiny little person on the other end of the phone who was trying to control her anger with me about the Fabergé egg comment, Gracie Blanche. What she lacked in height, she's only four feet eleven inches, she more than made up for it with tenacity. She was downright scary when she was focused on something.

Deep down, and I was never going to admit this to her, I actually have a lot of fun teasing her but I'm always there for her. These silly antique shows were her latest hobby and what's a friend for if you can't help support your friends in their latest endeavors.

"Because," apparently, she had gotten herself under control with the deep breathing exercise, "Anne and Chauncey like this area and they probably think they can help to bring in tourists which will help our economy."

I detected a somewhat guilty tone in her voice.

"Have you talked to them yet?" I asked.

"Oh, I'm sure they'll be agreeable to showing off their egg," Gracie Blanche said defensively. "After all, they do winter here."

"What does their being a snowbird have anything to do with displaying an egg?" I asked.

She harrumphed, "Well, if they come here to live for several months, I'm sure they want to promote our area." A slight pause, "And their egg."

"Wait! You mean you haven't even *talked* to them yet and you're already making plans for *their egg*?!" I was almost shouting. "Gracie Blanche, you can't do things like that!"

Apparently, she could, and she did.

CHAPTER 2

Gracie Blanche also hung up the phone on me. I said a few choice words about her, apologized to her dead mother in heaven, and called my office.

"Hey, Parker." My assistant, Missy, rarely had a bad or unpleasant day, even when I fired her. I did that about once or twice a year. She ignored me and continued to show up for work.

"Hey, yourself. By any chance..."

"Yes, Gracie Blanche emailed me a poster for the Full Moon Spring Solstice Antique Show showing a Fabergé egg as the featured item."

I let loose with a string of words. None of them nice and none that should be repeated in polite company...although they were commonly heard in Atlanta.

She ignored me and my outburst. "Rhonda Jean called and said you're invited to a birthday party on the twenty-fourth and you have to be there. Those were her words exactly."

Well, that jerked a knot in my tee shirt. Since I work for myself and I work from home frequently, I don't bother to dress up in anything fancy. Usually I wear jeans and a tee shirt of sorts. My attire could be called Po'thole chic or Atlanta homeless or my personal favorite, computer geek chic. Take your pick.

"Ah, what does she mean by that?" I cautiously asked.

Missy laughed, "That's exactly what she said you'd say. She said it was for Misty Dawn's birthday and that she had asked specifically for you to be there. Apparently, you're Misty Dawn's new BFF."

I groaned. Really? I had to go back to Po'thole three times in less than a twelve-month period of time? God hated me, I was sure of it. I was being punished for all of those nasty comments I've made over the years about that godforsaken little town; although maybe it was because of my less-than-desirable comments about the Baptists. I kind of suspected some of them might have a direct hotline to God and dialed Him directly when they heard some of my more choice comments.

"Well, she did save your life, Parker, the last time you were down there." Missy was nothing if efficient in reminding me of that.

"I guess I could go." Enthusiasm was not laced amongst those words. "What happens if I decide not to go?"

"Rhonda Jean said if you weren't down there two days prior to Misty Dawn's birthday she's going to hunt you down like a bad puppy dog, find you, and drag your fanny down there." She paused, "Probably not a good thing for you to ignore them, Parker. I'd hate to report you missing after three days."

I exploded. "What?! You're in on it with them?! Missy, you're fired!"

She laughed, "Yeah, whatever. I think you secretly like going down there. Let's face it, you're always the center of attention when you go."

"It's not the type of attention I want though!"

"Is Joe D. back yet?"

Okay, that stopped me in my tracks for a moment. Joe D. Savannah, owner of We Make Money, CPAs and my first love boyfriend, had taken off to the Virgin Islands with now wife number three. While he had always professed his undying love to me, he did have a nasty habit of marrying other women.

I mumbled something and took another sip of my coffee.

"Parker, I can't hear you," Missy singsonged.

"No! He's married...again. I don't expect to hear from him." I couldn't quite figure out my and Joe D.'s relationship. He always claimed I was his one true love and the only reason why he kept marrying other women was because I wouldn't marry him, or so he claimed.

The part about my not wanting to marry him was true. He wanted to live in Po'thole until he had calculated the last digit on someone's tax return. I wasn't remotely interested in spending my life in some stinking small sleepy town. I had a life to live.

Plus, I like large cities. I like the culture, the arts, the theater, the concerts, the different thought processes. Dare I even say it? I don't even mind the traffic in Atlanta. Of course, my office is only about fifteen or twenty minutes away from my condo and that's nothing in terms of getting to work in a large metropolitan area.

A fifteen or twenty-minute drive in Po'thole constituted going from one end of the county to the other. As enticing as that might be to some folks, it held absolutely no appeal to me. My brain probably looks like a fidget spinner when I'm there. I was always waiting for a car or even a truck to dart in front of me and see how close they could introduce their back bumper to my front end and claim it was mating season for vehicles.

However, I digress. Joe D. started seeing someone shortly after he had come to Atlanta for a 'high school reunion' with me. I don't understand that but whatever.

I had to give him credit where credit is due, he did have a way with women. They flocked to him like vultures do to fresh road kill. The good news is that Joe D. never procreated with any of his wives.

I strongly suspected the reason why the women married him was because they either thought he had a lot of money, he does but he's cheap, cheap, cheap, or they thought they were going to become part of Po'thole's movers and shakers group.

The first gal he married was the Miss Cabbage and Potato Queen. Nothing like getting hitched to a gal whose idea of fun is driving a John Deere tractor across rows of cabbage and potatoes and not getting thrown off. That matrimonial bliss lasted all of about six months when she discovered Joe D. wasn't going to pay for her to go to dental school.

The good news was she did have higher aspirations in life. The other news is she's a 'dancer' at a gentlemen's club in Jacksonville and putting herself through dental school utilizing that creative method. Where there's a will, there's a way.

Wife number two apparently was swept off her feet by the smooth-talking CPA. Yes, contrary to most certified public accountants having the personality of a thick piece of paper, Joe D. is cute as a button and has a very outgoing personality.

Of course, it helped that her daddy owned the four largest new car dealerships and three of the 'we tote the note' dealerships in town. Joe D. had been trying to get his business for years. I guess marrying his daughter was as good a way as any for getting the business.

She was cute in a sort of small town, inbred way. Unfortunately, she caught Joe D. in bed with her best friend and maid of honor only two months after the very expensive wedding her daddy had thrown for her. Joe D. had told him the wedding was a tax write-off because he was entertaining existing and potentially new customers, so it was elaborate.

Daddy quietly got her marriage annulled but kept Joe D. as his CPA. There's no justice for females in Po'thole.

Joe D. apparently decided the pickings were getting slimmer and slimmer in town so he turned to the internet, Intentional International Romance, to meet the future Mrs. Savannah. Turns out she was a Norwegian beauty who desperately wanted to come to America and become a citizen.

She got her wish within ninety days and they were apparently honeymooning in the Virgin Islands during my last escapade to Po'thole. I hadn't heard from him and didn't really want to because that would mean he'd be back to hounding me on the phone and wanting to have another 'reunion.' Not this time.

Missy broke into my thoughts. "Parker, do you want to drive down in your car or do you want to take the party wagon?"

My eyes crossed, I shuddered, my hands started shaking, acute stomach spasming occurred. I knew in my heart of hearts I was going back to Po'thole even though every fiber of my being was screaming, "No!"

Call it God, master of the universe, a cruel twist of fate, call it whatever you want but apparently the black hole of that godforsaken little town did not want to let me loose and kept trying to suck me back into its vortex of crazy people. It was like the town had attached invisible Velcro to me and I could only go so far before I was snatched back.

Let me be fair and say Atlanta has its fair share of folks who are a fingernail shy of being mentally competent, but they didn't try to involve me in their day-to-day life. They also didn't try to have me killed on a regular basis. Well, driving in Atlanta doesn't count.

"The party wagon," I mumbled. The party wagon was a converted RV that was tricked out with every electronics gear known to mankind. It was also armored to the hilt and a RPG, that's Rocket Propelled Grenade to those of you not in the know, couldn't penetrate its walls. I know. Someone tried that the last time I was in Po'thole, or maybe it was the time before. Whatever, I don't remember. I just remember someone trying to kill me in it and it withstood the attack.

I wasn't going to take any chances going back there. Who knew what crazy stuff might happen and I wanted to be protected.

"Do I dare ask where Misty Dawn's party is going to be?"

"Rhonda Jean said she'd pick you up." Missy was laughing. "You're just supposed to let her know when you're in your house."

A terrifying idea formed between my eyebrows.

"No! Absolutely not!"

"Absolutely not what, Parker?"

"They're NOT having Misty Dawn's birthday party at my house! NO, NO, NO!"

A soft sigh. "Parker, it's not at your house. It's not going to be at The Capt'n's Table or the karaoke place or the cabin in the woods that got blown up either. Rhonda Jean said it was some place where everyone could have a good time, be loud, and not have to worry about neighbors but, other than that, I don't know where it's going to be."

I'd like to tell you I relaxed, and the world was good. BUT I knew better. I also sloshed some of my nectar of the gods on my laptop keyboard since my hands were still shaking from the possibility of having the Lady Gatorettes at a birthday party at my house and I screamed, "NO!"

A snicker could be heard on the other end of the line. "I'll have another laptop delivered within an hour."

Already this wasn't starting out good and I hadn't even left Atlanta yet.

CHAPTER 3

While I wasn't wild about coming back to Po'thole, I was coming back for something that appeared to be fun and non-murder related. Plus, I was curious about this Fabergé egg Gracie Blanche had mentioned.

After my last visit, I did realize that the hormonally challenged, sugar-and-caffeine infused Lady Gatorettes – Mary Jane, Flo, Rhonda Jean, Myrtle Sue, and Misty Dawn – did have hearts of gold. Yes, it was deeply buried within each of them and it was definitely hidden under their Florida Gator tee shirts, but it was there. I had been the fortunate recipient of their having saved my life, several times, and discovered that they had a sense of humor I could relate to.

The Lady Gatorettes are a non-sanctioned division of the local University of Florida football booster club. The reason why they are non-sanctioned is because they got into a small altercation, okay the cops were called, many years ago and the powers that be in that club, yes everyone, decided the girls were not of the 'caliber' of members they wanted.

It also probably had to do with the fact that their husbands all worked blue-collar jobs and all of the members had white collar jobs and were management or business owners.

I will say it loud and hope that can I disavow ever saying these words in public, but the girls were just good plain old country girls and the term 'redneck' could be safely used on them. Professionals, even in small towns, do not appreciate some of God's more colorful characters in life.

The Lady Gatorettes are five hormonal women and have been best friends since elementary school. They wreak havoc everywhere they go. Believing that caffeine and sugar are an important daily ritual and a major food group requirement, they consume more than their fair share. People cringe and leave establishments when they enter.

Here's the short rundown on these gals.

Flo is a tall, slim waitress with long blond hair who is now on her sixth husband and makes one mean strawberry pie. Flo's reason for having so many husbands was because not one of them appreciated and loved the Gators as much as she did.

"Humph," she sniffed. "If my husband doesn't have a clue as to who the quarterback is, what type of offense the Gators are running, and who the coaches are, then what good is he to me?"

She also only dates men when it is not football season and that probably explains why she's never noticed that's why they knew nothing about Gator football. The ladies do not want company, including their husbands, bothering them on Saturday's game day, which explains why Flo only dates during the off-season.

Mary Jane, a very attractive brunette way back when, went to Atlanta for a weekend with some out-of-town cousins upon graduating from high school and upon her return has never seemed quite right. There has been much speculation that she indulged in some cheap street pharmaceuticals and that was the reason why she's just never been quite right upon her return. No one knows for sure—she's never explained—and her out-of-town cousins disavow knowledge of anything. They also have never visited her ever again.

Apparently not realizing New York City is bigger than Atlanta, she moved there for a brief moment in time. She thought she was in love with the city that never sleeps at night, changed her mind after a year, and came back. She's still a redneck but now has an educated palate. She also dates guys that she meets on the

Internet. While the rest of the Lady Gatorettes occasionally scold her for surfing for men on the Internet, they are all secretly envious of her.

She also keeps track of Joe D.'s latest profile on dating sites. His latest profile always creates a great deal of merriment amongst the girls when she finds a new one. She refuses to admit to being a stalker. Her version is she wants to make sure she doesn't show up on his "you might be a match" notification list.

What's my take on him going to dating sites? Hey, go for it! I totally get that Po'thole doesn't have a plethora of cute, intelligent women to choose from. Male pickings are even slimmer.

Myrtle Sue, a little dark-haired fireplug of a woman, is a domestic goddess. She knows every recipe that has ever been on the Food Network. She also surfs the Internet constantly looking for new information and statistics on the Gators. Her husband, while not understanding a single thing about the Gator football team and could care less, worships the ground his wife walks on. As long as he gets at least one hot meal a day he's a happy camper. He also has been known to brag that Myrtle Sue makes the best sand-wiches that could be eaten with one hand while driving his tractor out in the potato and cabbage fields.

Myrtle Sue has been known to boast that she had tracked her husband down during hunting season when he had "escaped"— her words—from the house without asking her permission. During hunting season, Southern boys don't believe it's necessary to ask their wives for permission to go hunting or explain why they go off in the woods with other men getting sweaty, nasty, dirty, stinky, and still don't have a dead animal to show for what they were doing over the weekend.

Apparently, it was that time of the month for Myrtle Sue and she had come home from a particularly bad time at Wal-Mart and discovered that her husband, the erstwhile J.W., had gone off for the weekend with the boys and left her a note saying he would see her Monday morning before he went to work. And, oh, yes, could he have clean clothes to wear on Monday?

Myrtle Sue saw red. She vowed that J.W. wouldn't have clean clothes for the remainder of hunting season because he'd made the fatal error of not saying "I love you" on his note.

After becoming a graduate of the 90-day Myrtle Sue School of Doing Your Own Laundry, J.W. now leaves notes with a great big "I Love You" on them.

Rhonda Jean is the trick play master. She knows every trick play that has been in a Gator game for the past thirty-five years. She also annoys the heck out of the coaches at Florida because she creates and sends in new trick plays every week during spring practice and the regular season. Rhonda Jean's fervent wish is that one of her plays will be used during a televised game and the Gators will run it in for a touchdown. So far it hasn't happened.

Her husband, Big T, short for Thomas the Third, is pleased as a pig in mud and mighty proud of his wife every time she receives a letter from the coaches. The fact that they are form letters doesn't bother him a bit. He just knows that one day one of his wife's plays will be used and then they will both be national celebrities.

Big T gave up chewing for dipping because dipping doesn't turn your teeth as brown and he's very proud of his big smile. Also, he says he doesn't want to look like a big old Southern redneck on national TV. The bad news is Big T poaches game and all the Fish and Game Commission people know him all too well and would like nothing better than to arrest him on national TV for poaching...gators.

Misty Dawn, the ringleader of this happy little group, stays in the Lady Gatorettes version of the Witness Protection Program aka WPP pronounced WIP, because local law enforcement still thinks she's killed up to six men. Let me point out that she's been cleared of all those charges by the FBI but apparently that's not good enough for the River County sheriff Dewitt Munster, yes that's really his name, and he's a TV-Barney Fife look alike. He wants to put her in jail so badly that he's been known to run a red light or two thinking he's spotted her. She's still roaming around freely and waves at him when she sees him going in the opposite direction. It drives him crazy.

Misty Dawn was so named because that's what the morning looked like the day she was born, and her mother took that as a naming sign. She sends encouraging cards and notes to all of the football players who play in each game. She was tickled pink when one of the players mentioned on national TV that it was her cards and letters that helped him during the difficult ordeal of his brother being arrested for dog fighting.

Misty Dawn, unfortunately, isn't quite as dainty as what her name might indicate. She has the vocabulary of a cross-country truck driver. And, oh, yes, she has a very short fuse on a very hot temper. The woman carries grudges like Christians forgive sins.

It's too bad that Misty Dawn didn't join the Navy. Swift, silent, and deadly, she would've made a natural Navy SEAL. She thinks her husband John Boy walks on water. He almost did the last time I was here because he failed to tell her about some of the riverfront development plans.

John Boy works construction and is afraid of no one except for his wife; however, he absolutely quivers when she walks in the house when she has that death-to-the-world glint in her eye.

If he doesn't let her vent when she gets mad, she goes out to the chicken house and they end up eating chicken for a month. Her record for killing chickens when she's in a state of anger is fifteen. As he confided to J.W. one night over beer, he was mighty happy he didn't have pigs or cattle on his ranchette because Misty Dawn might kill them all when she gets mad.

I wasn't exactly sure what kind of birthday party Misty Dawn was having so I was a wee bit nervous about coming back; however, I did know they liked me and I was sure they weren't planning on hiding my body out in the woods somewhere. Yes, that was a comforting thought. You'd have to know the girls to realize they're capable of doing anything and knowing one hundred percent I'm safe creates a great deal of peace for me.

Rolling into the driveway and inwardly sighing that I had a modular house where my childhood home had once been which I may have inadvertently blown up by accident the first time I came back to Po'thole and I sure wasn't going to admit to that, when I saw Bill Webble, my elderly neighborhood, hobbling over.

"Who's there? You don't have any business on that property!" He hoarsely shouted. Bless his heart. At least he was trying to look out for my property.

"Hey, Bill," I waved as I was getting out of the party wagon.

He stopped in his tracks, muttered something, waved his cane at me, and toddled on back in his house.

I hoped this was a good omen of my stay but, alas, it was not to be.

CHAPTER 4

The delicious aroma of freshly brewed coffee wafted gently in the house when I walked in. I inhaled it deeply. I doubt anybody or anything was ecstatic as I was to discover there was coffee waiting for me. Somehow Missy had once again made me feel right at home even though she was hundreds of miles away.

Reacting like Pavlov's dog, I headed for the coffee cup on the counter and ignored everything else. I was a woman on a mission, I wanted that coffee NOW. If anyone was going to kill or sabotage me, this time would be their best bet.

Yes, I am a coffee addict, and I am not going to attend any twelve-step program. Why? Because I have absolutely NO intentions of ever giving it up.

My charming personality, already a little on the wonky side, would slide over the edge of so-called normal society and turn me into someone you'd see on the national news...and not in a good way.

Sipping the nectar of the gods, I cautiously looked around to see if someone else had been living here while I was in Atlanta. Nope.

Finally noticing there was a note on the counter, I inhaled another big gulp before I read it.

"*Hi, Parker, the coffee was made at three twenty and Missy said you'd be here by three twenty-five. Glad you're here. I'll pick you up Friday morning at ten. Your shirt is hanging on the cabinet door. Go Gators! Rhonda Jean*"

I chuckled. Because I had been so focused on getting the cup of coffee I hadn't noticed that there was a nice, new Gator shirt hanging on one of the kitchen cabinet doors. I was touched because it was actually in my size.

My favorite song, Pink's 'So What', went off on my cell phone. I must ooze some type of strange pheromone when I entered the city limits that only natives can detect because it never fails the minute I'm back here, it seems everyone and their brother knows I'm back.

"Gracie Blanche, how did you know I was back?" I was laughing as I answered the phone, carefully looking at caller ID first.

"Because I passed you on the street a few minutes ago which, I'd like to point out, you totally ignored me and..."

"I didn't see you," I protested. I also rolled my eyes, but she couldn't see that.

"I decided to give you a few moments to get settled in before I called you."

"Yeah, okay. What's going on?"

"Have you met Anne and Chauncey Livingstone?"

"You mean the folks with the Fabergé egg that you're going to show off at the Full Moon Spring Solstice Antique Show and who you haven't even asked yet? Those folks?" My voice was dripping with sarcasm.

"They'll do it when I explain how important it is to our community." Gracie Blanche huffed.

"By the way, how did you find out they had a Fabergé egg in the first place?" Inquiring minds wanted to know, and especially mine.

"We're friends on Facebook and I saw Chauncey standing next to one at an antique show in Maine."

I snorted, "You know that's a bit of a stretch to think they might actually have a Fabergé egg, don't you? He may have just had his picture taken with it."

"Whatever. I'll ask him for sure when I see him later."

"Does he know about this?"

"I said I'd ask him later!" Great, Gracie Blanche had her hackles up on her four-foot eleven frame. She could give Attila the Hun a run for his money when she got mad.

"Where?"

"Where, what?" She icily replied.

"Where are you springing all of this on him?" I started to laugh. "Knowing you, it will be in a public place to make it difficult for him to turn you down. In short, you will try to embarrass him into it."

Once again, she started doing her deep breathing exercises while I poured another cup of coffee. I was grinning.

"It's trivia night at Mugsy Malone's and they always go there on Thursday nights when they're in town." Gracie Blanche was grinding her teeth.

I laughed. "See you there. I'll be protecting them from you."

She disconnected the phone and it rang again almost immediately.

"Parker."

"What, Missy?" I drank some more coffee.

"Did you leave Potus in the party wagon?"

My cup stopped halfway to my mouth. I slammed it down on the countertop and barreled out the door. As much as I love dogs, occasionally, I forget about Potus. I ripped open the RV door and he bounded down the steps. Did his business on the party wagon's tire, I didn't even want to think what that meant from a psychological standpoint, and then looked up at me with those condemning German Shepherd eyes.

"I forgot, I'm sorry," I weakly said.

He glared at me for a moment, wagged his tail and marched into the house. Apparently all was forgiven. With the exception of his mad love affair with Misty Dawn and the toleration of the Lady Gatorettes, Potus did protect me.

Fortunately, or unfortunately, he had absolutely no qualms about letting any of them into my house. That I could live with but his not even making a bark or a growl when they were in the house completely unnerved me something awful, particularly if I happened to walk out into the living room with no clothes on and they were there. 'Bad doggie' had absolutely no effect upon him.

I decided to go to the weekly trivia night at the local sports bar and I was only partially teasing Gracie Blanche about protecting Anne and Chauncey. She could be relentless when she wanted something. I had briefly met Anne and Chauncey a couple of times when I was in Po'thole before but really didn't know them other than to wave in passing.

Looks like I was going to have a fun evening. If I had only known.

CHAPTER 5

M ugsy Malone's sounded like it should be a pizza type place. It wasn't. It was a sports bar with all sorts of gangster type memorabilia all over the walls. The servers, god forbid I call anyone a waiter or a waitress because that is sooo politically incorrect, wore black pants, black suspenders, long sleeve white shirts with red armbands and a red string tie, with little black aprons and black Dr. Scholl's non-skid sneakers.

In short, this is considered fine dining in Po'thole. For some of these folks, the uniform was the nicest thing they owned.

Surprisingly, the décor was reasonably bright and cheery despite seeing grisly crime scene black-and-white photos plastered up on the walls. I guess since the photos were from the '30's then it shouldn't upset your appetite.

Let me be fair and say the really grisly ones were plastered high on the wall where it would be difficult for kids to see them. The standard tommy guns and 1930's memorabilia covered the rest of the walls.

The ubiquitous greeting of "Hi, I'm Sarah, and I'll be your server for tonight. What can I get you?" rubs raw on my nerves. They're either annoying perky, probably graduating from the Katie Couric School of Perkiness or the flat one-note 'I'd rather not be here' tone. Sarah graduated the perky school with high honors. Katie would be so proud.

"Do you have any coffee beers?" I did my best to smile sweetly.

It was like watching Bambi in the headlights. Her eyes opened wide, they blinked furiously, the smile slipped from her face, and you could see various facial expressions flitting across her face, ranging from the 'I don't have a clue' to 'is this a trick question' to 'how am I supposed to answer this'?

"Ah, um, let me check for you." She backed up and did a wonderful three-point turn heading for the inner sanctum of Mugsy's for assistance. The military would have been proud of her turn.

While I was waiting on her to return, at least I hoped she'd return, the table-top tri-folds brightly announced the trivia contest would start at seven. Glancing around I noticed the sports bar was starting to fill up. Spotting Anne and Chauncey coming through the door, I waved for them to come over and join me.

Anne turned her head to Chauncey, said something, he glanced over at me, shrugged slightly, and they turned their steps towards me.

"Hi, guys," I stood up. "Would you like to join me? I understand y'all are killer trivia night players and this is the first time I've come down for it."

"Sure, that sounds like fun," said Anne sliding into the booth on the opposite side of me. She had a big smile on her face. Chauncey handed Anne his backpack and slid in next to her.

Sarah popped back over about that time. Ignoring me for a moment, she said, "It's so nice to you again. What would you like to drink?"

I interrupted her. "Chauncey, I'm getting a coffee beer. Would you like one? The first round is on me."

A happy smile broke across his face. "Sure, that sounds fine."

Anne ordered a hot tea.

Sarah turned back to me. "I checked. We just got in Coffee Bender by Surly Brewing Company and it's supposed to be really good. Would you like two of those?"

"Yes." It was the best of both worlds, having the nectar of the gods in an adult foamy liquid libation. Life was good.

Anne and Chauncey had a beautiful aura surrounding them. The little I knew about was they had traveled a great deal, seen much, made little to no judgments on anyone, accepted folks as they are, and were very happy people. We won't talk about me.

Anne was an energetic, thin, medium tall, mature lady with curly silver hair with a few streaks of black thrown in for good luck. Chauncey had brown puppy dog eyes, was a more puckish, professor-ish looking gentleman with an impish grin under a white bushy mustache and had a thick shock of snow white hair he kept contained under a Bora Bora Booney hat.

As Chauncey and I hoisted our mugs along with Anne's cup of tea, I spotted Gracie Blanche barreling across the floor, heading toward us like a heat-seeking missile. She slid into the space next to me in the booth. Although I thought sitting in the middle would dissuade her from sitting down, I was wrong. Because she was not quite the height of short grown women, she fit fine on the tiny little bit of space I wasn't occupying.

"Hi, Anne and Chauncey." She ignored me. They glanced at me, I rolled my eyes upwards. Gracie Blanche couldn't see my eye-roll and they turned their attention to her.

"You know the annual Full Moon Spring Solstice Antique Show is the first week in April, right?"

Anne and Chauncey exchanged a cautious glance. Gracie Blanche plowed on, ignoring their look.

"I'm in charge of it," she smiled enthusiastically. I've seen professional sales-people who weren't this good. "I heard you have a Fabergé Egg and we would like to make it the star of the show! In fact, I took the initiative and had some posters made up so you could see what it would look like."

She unrolled the poster in her hand and spread it out on the table. She was looking at them with the assurance that it was a done deal. In sales, this is known as the assumptive close.

I had immediately noticed when Gracie Blanche was unrolling the poster that Anne's eyes had narrowed, and not in a good way. This was going to be interesting to see how this played out.

"What makes you think that?" Chauncey softly asked. "What makes you think I have one of those eggs?"

"Well, I saw a picture of you on Facebook standing next to it."

"Ah, well, I was standing next to it an antique show and a friend took my picture, tagged me on it, and posted it on Facebook."

"Okay, I get that," Gracie Blanche said, "but you still haven't answered my question. Do you have a Fabergé egg? I want to feature it at our antique show in April."

"No."

"No, what, Anne? No to the..."

"Oh, my, Gracie Blanche, no to everything." Turning to me, Anne said, "Parker, we might have to do trivia night another time with you."

Gracie Blanche, not having the sense God gave a goose, ignored Anne's gentle admonishment and said, "Why not? This would be great for our community! We could get national publicity..."

"No, Gracie Blanche! What part of them telling you 'no' did you not understand?" I was irritated. Of course, I had an ulterior motive. I wanted the Livingstones to see me as their savior from Gracie Blanche and they just might tell me if they actually have a Fabergé Egg. Yes, I'm just as nosy as the next person.

For those who aren't aware of the significance of an honest-to-goodness real Fabergé Egg, grab a cup of coffee, and see why I wanted to know if they have a genuine Fabergé. Owning an egg is equivalent to owning a priceless piece of history.

Peter Carl Fabergé was a Russian master jeweler and became known for his elaborate and intricate designs of jeweled Easter eggs he created for the Russian Tsars. He is particularly known for the ones he created for the Tsars Alexander III and Nicholas II. Yes, the same Nick II of Anastasia and Rasputin fame.

Fabergé created two Easter eggs a year for the royal family, one for the Tsar's mother and one for his wife. I'm taking a wild guess here but if mama, both of them, didn't get her egg there wouldn't be any happiness in the palace.

Anyway, they were dubbed the Imperial Easter Eggs. Each egg took approximately a year or more to make because of the intrinsic detail and the special surprise that was hidden inside the egg itself.

It's not the jewels that make the eggs valuable, it's the incredible attention to detail and the craftsmanship involved.

Here's where it gets really interesting if indeed Anne and Chauncey did have a genuine Fabergé, the real question becomes how and why do they have one? It seemed a little strange that these two people would have one. Usually you only find the eggs in a museum somewhere.

Since record keeping was a little dicey back then, what with the Russian Revolution and all, the actual number of Fabergé Imperial Easter Eggs created isn't exactly known. It's believed to be fifty, but it could be fifty-one or fifty-two and it's widely believed that only forty-three are still in existence but that's not a sure thing either.

Since only forty-three are suspected to have survived, then how did they get one? Why do they have one? Are they part of Russian nobility? If so, what were they doing here in the United States? And, lastly, why on God's green earth would they ever want to have it front and center at a little town's antique show?

What if one of these exquisite eggs has been passed down from generation to generation in one family? I would think it difficult to keep something like that a secret but those folks who are very wealthy do tend to keep things like that to themselves or it is only know in certain social circles. Not being mean, but I didn't think Anne and Chauncey fell into either of those categories.

My mind was dancing with all of the possibilities, playing the what if game about the Fabergé egg.

"Gracie Blanche," said Chauncey quietly. "The Tsarina has spoken."

"Yeah, but..." she protested.

"Go away, Gracie Blanche." I snapped. "Go annoy someone else but you gotta leave."

She finally turned her head to face me. I felt myself crumbling inside while I kept my face impassive although my heart was racing and my stomach was doing the dance of the seven fat ugly women.

I'm pretty sure if she ever came face-to-face with the devil, he'd back down in a heartbeat. Me? I was hoping all of my internal organs would stay intact and I wouldn't turn into a human grenade and explode everywhere. I didn't much think Sarah, our perky server, would appreciate having to clean up dead human debris.

It was the longest five seconds of my life. Gracie Blanche continued to glare at me before she slid out of the booth, didn't say anything to any of us, and marched out the door.

Chauncey started to chuckle. "You know, I thought she was going to explode. Glad she left."

I nodded. We enjoyed another beer, ate the standard sports bar food, and played trivia night as a team. We didn't win first place, but we did come in third which was good enough for another round of beer.

Since I knew Anne and Chauncey walked everywhere when they were in town, I offered to give them a ride home. It wasn't particularly late, but I hated the thought that they had to walk two miles home. They accepted and we continued to shoot the breeze and get to know each other.

Inquiring minds are probably asking, did I say anything to them about the Fabergé Egg or ask if they were Russian nobility? The answer is no. I wanted to build up the know, like, and trust factor...then I would ask them.

CHAPTER 6

"I told you having your picture taken with the egg and then putting it up on Facebook was going to create problems, Chauncey." Anne mildly admonished him as she twirled her tea bag in a cup of hot water. "I do wish you hadn't done that."

"Well, I didn't know that Emma was going to post the picture with me, Uncle Chauncey, and the egg on Facebook. Taking it to the antique show was okay because no one really believes an authentic Fabergé Egg would be in Maine, much less our small hometown."

"Yes, well, with social media someone might want to track it...and us...down to see if it's real. That's opening up a lot of doors from the past, doors that I thought we agreed to leave closed." Anne shook her head. "I don't know if I'm willing to go through all of this again."

Chauncey just nodded his head. In one sense, he was excited about getting possible answers to long held questions but, in the other sense, was this opening up doors to possible violence? At his and Anne's age, he wasn't sure if he wanted to go through a lot of toil and tribulation anymore. They had both left that life many, many years ago.

He vaguely wondered why he agreed to have his picture taken next to the Fabergé Egg in the first place. Was he toying with the universe or tempting something worse than fate?

Anne was right. There were certain doors that were closed from their past. Doors that, if opened, could wreak havoc on the peaceful life they had come to enjoy and one that they had carefully cultivated.

They both quietly wondered if they were willing to start a new life elsewhere...again.

CHAPTER 7

Hearing some giggling as I was struggling to push away the cobwebs from my eyeballs the next morning, the delicious aroma of freshly brewed coffee fired off a pleasurable synapse in my brain of joy and happiness.

Someone grabbed my hand and put a coffee mug handle in it. Wow! Service in bed? How wonderful! Wait! Did I inadvertently sleep with someone last night? I knew I hadn't been drinking heavily, Chauncey was married, way older than me, and married men weren't an option. A girl has to have her morals after all.

Did someone drop through the ceiling? I cautiously opened one eye and discovered all of the Lady Gatorettes, minus Misty Dawn, hovering over my bed with big smiles on their faces.

Potus was standing next to the bed wagging his tail. He had a love affair with these crazy women and did absolutely nothing to announce when they were in my house. Some watch dog he was turning out to be. The bad news is he only acted like this in Po'thole. In Atlanta, he would have killed anyone trying to get in my condo.

"Today is Misty Dawn's birthday and we came by to pick you up for the party." Rhonda Jean was absolutely giddy with excitement. Me? Not so much since I hadn't consumed my first cup of coffee even though I was holding it in my hand.

Struggling to sit up in bed, I wondered vaguely if this was how a mother felt upon first awakening and discovering all of her progeny offspring standing, sitting, climbing, and laying on the bed with her. If so, I was glad I didn't have children.

"Ladies, you're not supposed to pick me up until ten o'clock and," I squinted my eyes to see the digital clock on the nightstand, "it's only eight thirty. Why are you so early?"

"See? I told you so." Myrtle Sue was smug in her assessment of my early morning less-than-cheerful attitude. Unfortunately, she was right. I absolutely DEPLORE being awaken before nine and preferably ten in the morning. I'm a night person. Without that first delicious cup of coffee warming all of my molecular cells from my mouth down to my toes, I was never going to be voted Miss Congeniality. Sad to say, I was probably never going to be voted that later in the day either. My basic personality is what is probably considered an acquired taste, at least according to the few friends I have.

Flo stuck a doughnut in my empty hand since the other one was holding the coffee up. "We know it takes you a few extra minutes to get ready and..."

"Although why it takes you so long when you dress like we do, I don't understand," snickered Mary Jane. I glared at her. She was right, I just didn't like it being pointed out.

"Anyway," Flo continued, "we wanted to help you get going a little faster than normal."

Rhonda Jean was eyeing my doughnut with the intensity of a starving dog seeing a steak for the first time and knowing that if he acted quickly enough, he could get the steak and wolf it down before anyone could punish him. Realizing that I valued my fingers staying attached to the rest of my hand much more than I did the tastiness of the doughnut, I offered it to her. She popped the whole thing in her mouth.

"Aw right, everybody out so I can shower and get dressed."

"How long do you think that's going to take you?" asked Flo.

I glared at her and she looked over the top of my head and continued to smile sweetly. I wasn't going to win.

"Fifteen minutes," I growled.

As they were trooping out of the room, Flo turned back around. "We're timing you." I threw a pillow at her, but she had already closed the door.

Thankfully we were using Rhonda Jean's monster SUV to take us to wherever it was we were going. I was grateful they didn't want to ride in the party wagon. I was taking a wild guess that whatever we were doing involved barbeque and an all-day affair of drinking beer. I couldn't have been any more wrong.

We drove out to Horseshoe Landing where a very nice houseboat was moored about fifty yards offshore. When I realized that's what we were going on, fear and trepidation set in. I started to perspire heavily. Why? I don't swim very well and there are a TON of gators and poisonous snakes in the St. Johns River. I didn't want an up close and personal introduction to them.

Sad to say, I had not noticed the two canoes on top of Rhonda Jean's SUV. The girls were busy getting them down.

"Ah, are we're going to have to go in those things?" I nervously asked. I could just see me getting baptized unceremoniously and, without a minister present, I wasn't sure this would be considered a sanctioned event by whatever religious denomination the girls belonged to.

"We're putting you in a life jacket," said Flo. She raised an eyebrow at me, a talent I truly envied in others because I couldn't do it. I involuntarily shuddered.

She laughed, "Parker, if we wanted you dead, you'd be dead by now."

A comforting thought, not, and one that had already occurred to me. Holding my breath the entire time we wobbled out to the houseboat, it didn't help my nerves one bit to see four water moccasins swimming around the canoe. Unlike a lot of other snakes, cottonmouths swim with their heads fairly high out of the water. They look like tiny submarines with a baby periscope coming out of the water when they're swimming.

Since it is Spring and mating season, there were quite a few of them swimming in the river. While it obviously didn't bother any of the Lady Gatorettes, it was another nature nightmare come to life for me. I wanted to go home, back to Atlanta. I like the concrete jungle. There's a reason why I moved away from all of this nature...I don't like it!

As we gently bumped into the houseboat, a number of helping hands pulled me on board where I quickly shed my life jacket. I was pleasantly surprised by what I saw on the top deck.

There was a beautifully set table, complete with real silverware and glasses. I guess I was expecting a redneck hoe down complete with a beer keg, roadkill hors d'oeuvres, chicken wings, and barbeque. I was actually a little nervous that this could easily turn into a major disaster, like with the girls jumping overboard and using the snakes as a ring toss game. I could not have been more wrong. This was as nice as anything I'd seen in Atlanta and I have been to a lot of upscale parties.

Mary Jane smiled when she saw me gaping at the decorations. "Yes, contrary to the image that we work so hard at, we do enjoy nice things...once in a while. I had it catered out of Jacksonville along with the boat.

"Misty Dawn really wanted you to be here for her party. And, before you ask, no, she isn't telling you which birthday it is. She just wants us to all have fun and relax."

Wow! The whiff of a baby gerkin pickle could have blown me off the top deck. This was truly amazing! Who knew the Lady Gatorettes might actually have some redeeming social graces? Of course, the day was young and the thought crossed my mind that the Florida Fish and Wildlife Conservation Commission, formerly known as the Florida Freshwater and Game Commission, might be sitting out in the river somewhere with a pair of binoculars on us waiting to see what trouble we might get into and what they could arrest us for.

Of course, the other standpoint was Misty Dawn technically still had a warrant out for her arrest and potentially they could arrest her. The local sheriff, Dewitt Munster, known in most circles as Dimwit, had issued it six murders ago. All of the evidence was circumstantial at best and not worth pursuing, according to the county attorney, but Dimwit was convinced Misty Dawn was an Aileen Wournos serial killer copycat. The FBI had told him the warrants were no longer enforceable, but Dimwit didn't care. He thought Misty Dawn didn't know about that minor technicality. She did and had her illustrious attorney Sophia Poppy on speed dial. Of course, I seriously doubted the Lady Gatorettes would ever let their leader be arrested and taken to jail.

Misty Dawn didn't want to take a chance proving her innocence by turning herself in because, well, she scared a lot of people in River County and Po'thole with her charming personality. She was very concerned, on basic principles, that she'd be found guilty and thrown in jail, regardless of what the FBI said. Sophia Poppy had also assured her that she'd be okay, but Misty Dawn wasn't taking any chances.

If that ever happened, she had already vowed, she'd break out of jail and never be seen ever again. So, it was easier for her to stay away from and out of sight of Dewitt. There were enough redneck people in the area who believed she was being unfairly charged and they were more than willing to help her elude Dewitt. Not hard to do since he was Po'thole's version of Barney Fife from the old Andy Griffith television show back in the sixties.

The Lady Gatorettes suddenly started squealing and jumping and up down. Looking into the morning sun bouncing around on the surface of the river, I could see a pontoon boat approaching. It had mylar balloons tied all over it and they were whipping around like crazy because of the speed of the boat and the wind.

Misty Dawn was riding in the front of the boat much like Kate Winslet did in the Titanic movie. Then I heard it. Hard to believe but, yes, indeed, it was Celine Dion singing "My Heart Will Go On." Hearing that beautiful angelic song being sung by Celine did nothing short of making my eyeballs start to sweat. Looking at the other Lady Gatorettes, I could see they were overwhelmed as well. It truly was a magical moment.

Misty Dawn boarded the houseboat and all of the girls bowed to her as she walked the red carpet to her spot at the head of the table. While I would never ever normally say Misty Dawn looked regal in anything, I did have to admit she did exude a certain amount of charm and charisma wearing the always approved and favored orange and blue of the Gators as she sat down.

"Parker, I am so glad you could join us."

Say what?! Twice in one day someone could have blown me overboard with stinky bad breath. I wondered if this new-found camaraderie meant I was being inducted into the Lady Gatorettes. While it would be an honor, mainly because I have better sense than turning down a bunch of hormonal sugar-and-caffeine-infused women who know how to kill with their bare hands, it's not something I truly wanted to be a part of or even associated with on a regular basis.

"Thank you, Misty Dawn." Yes, I could be gracious when I needed to be. I was still curious as to why I was invited to her birthday party...unless...I was part of the entertainment.

"Do you know why you were invited to my party?"

I shook my head no. My heart started pounding. More fear and trepidation caused profuse sweat to roll down the middle of my back in waves. I wondered what would be a more painful death...the Lady Gatorettes or the poisonous deadly water moccasins? I really didn't want to find out.

"It's because you were nice to us and you didn't turn any of us in to Dimwit."

I smiled, and my heartbeat started to slow and return to normal. My shirt, however, could have been wrung out with as much moisture that had been absorbed. The Florida humidity doesn't count.

"So. What do you know about Anne and Chauncey's Fabergé Egg?"

Because I don't have a really good poker face, my eyes popped wide open and my mouth dropped open. "Say what? How do you know anything about that?"

Out of nowhere some female servers in black pants and white shirts appeared carrying beautifully arranged plates of lobster and designer-cut vegetables. Another server appeared and poured iced tea. Taking a sip of the ungodly sweet liquid, my brain was frantically trying to piece together this party, the Fabergé Egg, and what the Lady Gatorettes had to do with it, I inadvertently squinted my eyes shut and puckered up my mouth.

Flo laughed. "Too sweet for ya, Parker? You've been gone from home way too long."

"I don't normally drink sweet tea and I don't think I've been gone long enough," I snapped. "If I never had to come back here, it would be too soon for me."

Sweet tea basically sugar water with a small amount of brewed Lipton's tea...and, yes, it has to be Lipton's, is the preferred non-alcoholic drink of choice in the South. If you were a diabetic, one sip could send you into insulin shock and you'd be dead before the EMTs could arrive.

All heads whipped around to see what Misty Dawn would do and then their heads all whipped back around to me. It was like watching an exorcist movie except maybe I was the demonic one and didn't realize it.

Misty Dawn blinked. It was probably a special secret signal to Myrtle Sue because she said, "We heard through the grapevine..."

I snorted, "Probably Gracie Blanche."

She ignored me and continued, "That Anne and Chauncey have a Fabergé Egg and they're going to display it at the Full Moon Spring Solstice Antique Show."

"Why?"

"Why, what?"

"Why would they want to display a priceless Fabergé Egg at a no-nothing antique show out in the middle of nowhere?" I looked around the table. "Besides which, that picture of Chauncey on Facebook standing next to the egg doesn't mean he owns it."

Misty Dawn nodded her head in agreement. "True but what do you really know about Anne and Chauncey?"

I was puzzled. "What do you mean? I haven't lived here in a boatload of years. This is the third time I've come back in less than twelve months. That's three more times than I have been in the last twenty years. I know who they are because of Facebook and that they winter here but other than that, I know very little about them.

"What do *you* know about them?"

Misty Dawn grinned. "About the same as you, and I agree. Why would they want to bring a very expensive fancy Russian Egg to Po'thole much less put it in one of Gracie Blanche's antique shows? It doesn't make any sense."

We all had a very enthusiastic discussion while consuming vast quantities of lobster prepared three different ways. It was a very delightful afternoon and not once did any one of the ladies get out of control by over-consuming too much caffeine or sugar. Surprisingly, there was no alcohol served but then I remembered they didn't normally drink during the day. This was like a very nice ladies luncheon except that it was on the water on a houseboat. Then we heard the water police's siren go off about a hundred yards from the boat.

We had been aware of a boat approaching but hadn't paid the slightest bit of attention to it until that siren went off and we heard the bullhorn voice saying, "We are boarding your boat. Stand by."

Misty Dawn dropped to the floor and crawled into the main cabin. I knew there had to be a special hiding place for her, but I didn't want to know where and, more importantly, I knew we hadn't done anything wrong to warrant anyone boarding the boat except out of sheer harassment.

Both men boarded and were standing on the main deck demanding to see our driver's licenses.

After living in Atlanta for however many years and being pulled over by the cops for speeding on numerous occasions, I knew my rights.

"Officers, why do you need to see our licenses? We've rented a houseboat, we have a captain, there's no alcohol or firearms on board." I was praying about that last part because I strongly suspected there might be some weapons of mass destruction on board. "Why do we need to provide any documentation to you?"

The taller one said, "And you are?"

"Parker Bell."

They looked at each other. Then, "You are under arrest."

"For what?" I screeched. "I've been here all day."

Stress was an understatement. I hated this little town. Every time I came back here something awful happened...and usually not to my benefit. Anything that stressed me out could send me from being totally calm to exploding over the moon in a nano-second. Po'thole had that effect on me.

The taller one grinned. "Gracie Blanche said to tell you if you ever embarrass her again like you did the other night at Mugsy Malone's, she will and, let emphasize the word will, have you arrested."

I gritted my teeth. "You tell that short, little Neo-Nazi, Attila the Hun, she'd better stay far, far away from me or I'll have my attorney slap a stalking and harassment charge on her. Also, tell that nasty, little vertically challenged person not to ever call me again about anything. I. Am. Pissed. Off."

Laughing, they were about to get back in their boat, when I said, "By the way, did she pay you to do this or is she sleeping with one of you guys?"

If looks could kill, I'd be in the river with the snakes and gators but since looks don't kill and I had the Lady Gatorettes as witnesses, I knew I was safe. The men mumbled something, got back in their boat and took off.

I was still fuming and said several very unkind things about Gracie Blanche...all true but still unkind.

Misty Dawn, Flo, Myrtle Sue, Mary Jane, and Rhonda Jean all laughed. After a few moments, I did too.

"You know, I could make her life totally miserable while I'm here but," I noticed the gals looking at each other and sending some type of signal between them. "No! You guys don't do anything to her right now. I want to wait until the time is right."

They reluctantly nodded in agreement. I did notice they didn't look at each other when they nodded.

It did occur to me when I was at home taking a shower several hours later that maybe, just maybe, they might do something that would upset Gracie Blanche tremendously. *That* I was okay with. I just wanted her to leave *me* alone.

I set the coffee pot to start brewing at nine forty-five the next morning. Determining that I would have several cups of the delicious nectar of the gods before I hit the road back to Atlanta little did I know I'd be staying a lot longer than I had originally planned. Nothing ever seemed to go right when I came back to my old hometown. It was no different this time either.

CHAPTER 8

Pink's "So What" started playing on my cell phone at exactly nine forty-two a.m. I groaned. Cracking open one eye, I groaned even louder. I punched the talk button waiting for the onslaught of perkiness to emanate from my phone.

And there it was.

"Girl! You're in Po'thole and you didn't tell me? Shame, shame, shame!" Yep, it was my book agent extraordinaire Saffron Woo. No mama would ever give their child that birth name. I had it on good authority that Saffron's real name was Delilah Brooke, she was Jewish and from South Carolina. I didn't care if she was from Mars and hung upside down, she was a terrific agent and got me great deals on my books.

But, golly Moses, she was an early morning person, I wasn't, and I swear she's the one who taught Katie Couric the extremely annoying technique of being extremely perky at the ungodly morning hour of five. That's fine if you work in morning television, not great if you don't. Loved Saffron, hated her perkiness before ten a.m.

"How did you know I was here?" I groaned as I struggled to navigate my way through the bedroom door to the kitchen where my coffee had just started brewing. "You know if you waited just another five minutes, I'd have coffee in me and I'd be a lot easier to deal with." I grumbled.

"Parker, darling," she laughed. "If I did that, you'd ignore my calls because you could see your caller ID much better."

Reluctantly, I had to agree.

"So, what's the deal on this Fabergé Easter Egg?"

"What the heck is going on with this egg? Everybody in the world seems to know about it except me and yet I'm the one who's getting asked all the questions." I inhaled a mouthful of coffee.

"Apparently you're the conduit," laughed Saffron. "So, are you ready for me to pitch another book idea?"

"Nothing to pitch, Saffron. The only thing that's coming up is that Full Moon Spring Solstice Antique Show."

"No murders, no nothing?"

"Nope, not a thing, Saffron. This is a very calm trip and I'll be leaving either later today or first thing in the morning."

"What about the Fabergé Egg?"

What was the big deal about this egg?! Why were people getting so excited about it? It's not like Po'thole...or even all of northeast Florida...had a huge population of Russians who were trying to get a national treasure back. After all, the Soviet Union didn't exist anymore, and their government wasn't on a major search mission for the eggs as far as I knew. They were predominantly collector items of a bygone era. At least, that's all I knew about the Fabergé Eggs.

"Did Gracie Blanche call you? Is she trying to get you to ask me to ask Anne and Chauncey to put their egg, if they even have one, in that silly antique show of hers?" I demanded.

"Maybe."

That one-word answer from the chattiest person this side of normal told me everything and more than I wanted to know. It also meant the water police guys had told her what I had said. Good! I was now officially beyond irritated at Gracie Blanche. She could eat dirt and die as far as I was concerned about that antique show. I wasn't going to help her in the slightest.

In fact, I'd probably go out of my way and badmouth it to everyone I knew in town. Okay, that might only be a handful of people, BUT they were the right handful of people to spread the word.

"Saffron, you can tell that gossipy little person I'm going to tell everyone I know to stay away from the antique show. So there!" I took a deep breath. "Don't call me unless you have another book deal!"

Pushing the end button on my phone, I slammed it down on the countertop and slurped another big gulp of coffee.

I called Missy. "Hey, Potus and I are going to be leaving in the next couple of minutes and heading home. Anything going on?"

"Well, Anatoly Petrov called and wanted you to personally call him."

"Really? Anatoly Petrov? What about?" This could be big. While I had a number of various government agencies and a few other countries we did dark web security work for, I really didn't have any Russian ones. They tended to play everything very close to their vest and use their own people.

Anatoly Petrov was a Russian billionaire businessman with many rumored unsavory contacts. His office had contacted me several years ago about a possible business deal but nothing ever came of it.

"Do we have anyone who is fluent in Russian?" I couldn't think of any personnel who was fluent but, then again, my company had grown so rapidly that I really didn't know everyone anymore. Missy is the one who actually keeps me in the loop. We were still small, about fifty people and I didn't really run things any more on a day-to-day basis. We had an excellent checks-and-balance system in place. One that I could check on every single day if my little heart so desired, usually it didn't.

I had key people in place I depended upon and, unbeknownst to them, there was a backdoor in my system that Missy could and did check in on them on a regular basis. She was a lot more versed than anyone gave her credit for. I was happy no one thought she was anything more than my assistant.

"Parker, I think Andrew might be." I could hear her fingers tapping on the keyboard. "Yes, he was born Andrei Dubrovskaya but goes by Andrew Druber.

He anglicized his name, probably to fit in better. His family came to this country in 1980 when he was three. So, he's just turned thirty. His dad is a professor of economics at Berkeley and his mother teaches ballet here in Atlanta."

"So, they're divorced?" I asked.

"No, separated. Separated for about twenty years. The dad taught economics in Russia before coming over here and...Aha! Get this, his mother was a cultural attaché. She was an art historian."

"Are these guys sleepers?" Oh, great! I might have a potential Russian spy working for me. I might already have a leak within my company.

"Don't think so, Parker. His dad was quite vocal about the Russian government long before Andrew was born. Her, maybe, unless she was someone's mistress and got promoted to cultural attaché when they got tired of her...maybe as a reward or something."

"Is the dad actually Andrew's dad?" I was making another pot of coffee. Hey, I needed brain stimulation to process all of this information.

"Yes, it would appear so." Missy's fingers were still tapping merrily on the keyboard. It's amazing how much like music typing on a keyboard could sound like. "He got a job offer from Berkeley before ever putting in a request to emigrate from Russia. They were together for about ten years before she split and moved to Atlanta. She brought Andrew with her. Dad visited every other weekend until Andrew was eighteen."

"Wow! That had to be expensive on a professor's salary. What else was he doing, either on the side or once he got to Atlanta?"

"Um, shows that he and Andrew went to the zoo a lot."

"Drop box?"

"Don't know."

"How long has Andrew been with us?" Inquisitive minds need to know these things. Also, it might be a security issue for me and my company.

"He's been with us four years. Came on board after getting his master's in computer science. We're the only company he's ever worked for."

"I want you to..."

"Already on it. It'll take me the rest of the afternoon to get the voice transcriptions. This is assuming that neither one of them used burner phones."

"Last question..."

Missy interrupted me, "He's not involved in anything outrageously sensitive. I'm going to have him come in once we get off the phone and I'll ask him if he can speak Russian fluently. Then I'll ask him if he knows who Anatoly Petrov is. I've got the cameras set up behind my desk, he won't know they're there, and then I can get our guy to read the micro-expressions later. I've also got the thermal heat detectors set up so we can get the printouts on that as well."

"Alright, sounds good. I'm going to leave in the next thirty minutes and I should be home around eight. I'm not calling Anatoly back until I hear back from you. Later."

This was starting to get very interesting. Why would a Russian billionaire businessman call me? I strongly suspected it was something more than computer security he was interested in.

I called Anne and Chauncey to invite them to come to Atlanta any time. They were gracious and declined at this time. They liked the spring weather right here and then the first of June they were going to head back to Maine.

Who knew I'd be seeing them long before June?

CHAPTER 9

The good news is all I had to do was walk out of my house and into the party wagon. I could leave everything exactly the way it was in the house. I knew Missy would have someone clean the house while I was gone. I strongly suspected it was one of the Gatorettes but I didn't really want to know and I really didn't care. Since I never claimed to be Suzy Homemaker, I was just grateful someone else was doing it.

For all I knew it might be a hiding spot for Misty Dawn...and, surprisingly, that was okay with me. I was happy and singing because Potus and I were heading back to Atlanta. He was trying to pretend to sleep and I was trying to pretend I could sing on key. Celine Dion was never going to ask me to sing backup for her.

I was almost to Tifton, Georgia when Missy called me.

"Yo!" I was happy. That was about to change.

"Do you have a coffee with you?" This was not a good sign when Missy started off a conversation like that.

"Um, no, but there's an exit coming up and I can get one then."

"Do it and then call me back."

"How about giving me the bad news now and then I'll get the coffee?"

"Call me back once you have the coffee."

I groaned. This wasn't good. I pulled into one of those gigantic gas stations. You know the kind, the ones that look like the Atlanta airport with fifty million different hubs and lanes. All I wanted to do was get inside and get a coffee, not try to figure out which lanes were moving the fastest to the gas pumps. It kind of looked like the lines at Space Mountain at Disney World...hurry up and wait.

Finally, I decided to park behind a semi in the parking lot, figuring he was going to pull forward and not back up. For once in my life, I guessed right. Potus stood guard in the party wagon while I got the largest coffee the station had.

Punching my speed dial for Missy, I wondered what had happened. We did have secret key words to use if something really awful happened but since she hadn't used them, I was fairly sure the building and my company hadn't blown up.

"Parker, you have your coffee?"

"Yes."

"You're parked and not driving?"

"Yes."

"Okay, Andrew is definitely lying about something but it's probably not work-related. He's googled Anatoly ten times in the past three months. It's not on any regular day or time. It appears to be just on a random basis. I can't see anything in his work that would indicate he's communicating with him or anyone else.

"When I asked him if he spoke fluent Russian. He seemed surprised and then said he grew up speaking it at home. He was very quick to point out that he and his parents are naturalized citizens and that they love America.

"When I told him he was being considered to head up a new project, a Russian project, I thought I saw a micro-expression and then I later confirmed it. It appeared to be a stress reaction. Also, his body temperature elevated slightly. I'm not sure if these were positive or negative stressors.

"He admitted to knowing who Anatoly is but, when asked if his dad knew him personally, Andrew said he didn't think so.

"Parker, there is a possibility that his dad does know Anatoly because they are about the same age and they were in Moscow at the same time. It's also totally possible that Andrew does not know if his dad knows Anatoly."

"Missy, it just occurred to me. What is Andrew's father's name?"

"Hold on. It's Viktor Dubrovskaya."

Bells and whistles started going off in my head. I was stunned. "Are you serious?"

"Yes. Why? What's going on, Parker?"

"Wasn't he considered Russian nobility before coming to America? He has quite the reputation for understanding international economics and gives heavy duty speeches about it in front of the United Nations."

Whoa. Things were becoming increasingly interesting.

"Find out what month he came to this country and where he went before showing up at Berkeley. I'm betting you there is a two to three-month lag time in there somewhere."

My phone started beeping. "Hold on, Missy, I've got another call coming in.

"Parker Bell."

"Parker, it's Rhonda Jean. You've got to come back to Po'thole. It's bad, really bad."

I had never heard Rhonda Jean so upset but I didn't want to get taken in by another practical joke from Gracie Blanche.

"Yeah, why? What's really bad?" I was suspicious.

"Gracie Blanche, Myrtle Sue, and Flo have all been beaten up really bad and Gracie Blanche is on life-support. You've got to come back...And we can't find Misty Dawn either." She wailed.

"Why? What?" I was stunned. It was all I could do to keep from bursting into tears. Yes, Gracie Blanche could be a holy terror, but she would never hurt anyone. Why someone deemed it necessary to hurt her or any of the Lady Gatorettes was beyond me. I had an incredible sinking feeling in the pit of my stomach.

Then it occurred to me, I might be new the defacto leader of the Lady Gatorettes. I guess I should be honored but the thought did make me nauseous. Why? Really? Do *you* want to lead a bunch of hormonal sugar-and-caffeine infused women? Yeah, I didn't think so, and that's my answer too.

"Myrtle Sue and Flo went over to Gracie Blanche's to tell her to leave you alone. I got the panic signal from Flo's phone. Mary Jane and I went over there...and it was awful, Parker, it was just awful." Rhonda Jean sniffled. "There was blood everywhere. We had to call 9-1-1. They had to get all three ambulances to take them to the hospital."

Rhonda Jean took a deep breath. "Parker, we have it set up so that when the panic signal goes off it goes to all of our phones along with the GPS location. Plus, we also have a special signal for Misty Dawn and she's not responding.

"Before you ask, that signal can be located anywhere within sixty miles including her being out on the river. She's not answering. This isn't good. What has happened to Misty Dawn?"

Before I could stop the words from flying out of my mouth I said, "God help the poor sucker who has kidnapped Misty Dawn! She'll kill 'im if she has the chance."

"You wait until I tell Misty Dawn you made a joke about her!" snapped Rhonda Jean. "John Boy ain't gonna be too happy about that either!"

"Whoa, whoa!" I could just see my life ending at the hands of Misty Dawn. That was not a pleasant thought. Well, dying for any reason wasn't a pleasant thought in general.

"How long has it been since you've heard from her? How long does it normally take for her to respond to a panic signal?"

"It's been over an hour and everyone normally responds within ten to thirty seconds."

"Where's Mary Jane?" The Lady Gatorettes all needed to be accounted for. While Mary Jane was an outstanding cook and could weld a knife with the best of any television chef, I wasn't sure how she'd stack up against a crazed person or persons.

"She's hiding."

"Where, Rhonda Jean? I need to make sure she's safe too."

"She's in my SUV."

"What? How is she hiding?" It was like pulling teeth trying to get information out of her.

"She's under one of the seats."

I started to laugh. "Willingly or unwillingly?"

"I warned you about making fun of us."

"I'm not making fun of you guys. I'm just trying to figure out why you would hide Mary Jane in one of the seats."

"Because if something happened to me, there would be at least someone to take revenge on the sucker who killed me! We have to make sure at least one of us is alive. Even though we have all taken krav maga self-defense classes, we need to make sure at least one Lady Gatorette is alive at all times."

Okay, made sense to me. Revenge is best served on a cold platter and knowing these gals like I did, whoever hurt one of them was probably going to die a slow unnatural death.

"Have you called Dewitt and reported what happened?"

"Cops were called the minute all of the ambulances showed up. I think we need to put Myrtle Sue and Flo in protective custody."

"What about Gracie Blanche?"

"She's probably not going to make it, according to the EMTs." Rhonda Jean took a deep breath. "Parker, you really need to come back here. Gracie Blanche had a piece of paper in her hand and there's a name on it. I think it's French." What? That's weird. I was still trying to wrap my brain around three of my friends being beaten up and in the hospital. Okay, yeah, I guess I have to admit it. I do consider the Lady Gatorettes as my friends...friends who I always want to stay on their good side though.

"What's the name on it?"

"Anatoly Petrov."

You could have had a gnat blow on me and I would have fallen over.

CHAPTER 10

That name jolted me. What were the chances of having three friends in the hospital, a piece of paper with a Russian billionaire's name on it, and then receiving a phone call from him?

That was way too many coincidences...and I don't believe in coincidences.

Which reminded me, I still had Missy on hold. "Rhonda Jean, I'm heading back. It should take about two hours." I took a deep breath and said, "If y'all want to stay at my house until I get back, go ahead."

I was crossing my fingers she wouldn't do it.

Rhonda Jean said, "I've got to go home and fix Big T's dinner. Mary Jane can though."

Priorities. A brief moment of discussion and then, "Mary Jane says she'll have a nice dinner waiting on you so you don't need to stop at some truck stop and eat some of that nasty greasy food. I'll come on over later."

Oh, great! I had been thinking about going into the gas station again and getting some tacos to eat on the way back. Maybe Mary Jane wouldn't notice my taco breath if I ate some mints and, for sure, I'd eat her meal when I got back. A gal's got to keep her strength up, after all.

"Okay." I clicked over to Missy and discovered she had already disconnected me. Calling her back as I walked into the gas station, I eyeballed their fast-food selection and decided that two tacos from the national chain of Tacos R Great wouldn't kill me. I would, however, pay the price about an hour later with acute indigestion.

"Parker, what's going on?" Missy did sound concerned after I called her back.

I brought her up to speed on my and Rhonda Jean's phone call.

"Do you want me to order security for the girls? I can probably have someone there within an hour."

I cleared my throat, a truly ladylike thing to do. "If there are Russians involved, my first question is why, and my second question is are they professionals? If that's the case, it's truly overkill, no pun intended, in this area.

"Yes, on security. Make sure whoever you get isn't a run-of-the-mill security guard; otherwise, we're going to be having a ton of hurt people. What the heck is going on, Missy?"

"Maybe you should call this Anatoly Petrov guy and find out. Maybe he's behind it."

I snorted, "There's no reason why he should be. I think he's calling about us doing some computer work for him."

Surprisingly, I got through to Anatoly on the second ring. He must have given me his direct number. Usually on very high-profile people, I still have to go through a personal secretary or assistant to get to them.

"Mr. Petrov, this is Parker Bell returning your call." I could be very professional when I needed to. My dead mother would be so proud to know I retained some of her training for good manners.

"Ah, Ms. Bell, thank you for returning my call." His English was very good, a slight accent but I could certainly understand him much better than my tv cable company's "customer support" team based in India or from some planet in a solar system far, far away.

"I understand you know about a Fabergé Easter Egg being in Pothole." Yes, indeed, he did say Pothole and not Poat Hole or even Po Ho. What irritated me more was that he KNEW where I was, not a good sign. So much for me thinking I had a low profile or that I could be a great spy.

I was stunned. How did he know about that?

My voice was very clipped. "Mr. Petrov, I own a high-tech computer security company and I was under the impression that you might want to secure our services for a particular project."

A slight chuckle, one that caused the hair on the back of neck to stand straight up. "I am very aware of your services and how you have helped many different companies and countries with various problems; however, this is a personal call." He paused, "You may not be aware of this, but I collect Fabergé Eggs for my personal collection. In fact, I own the largest collection of Fabergés in the world."

I swear, I wish my lips would clamp down sometimes and refuse to let potentially acrimonious words slide out of my mouth and into open air where they could do a lot of damage. That didn't happen.

"Seems fitting that a Russian billionaire would collect Russian Fabergé Eggs," I retorted.

"It is part of our history, our culture, that our eggs be kept by Russians."

Did I have the sense to be quiet and see where Petrov might take the conversation? But, no, I did not.

"It would probably be nice if they were showcased where the Russian people could actually see them and appreciate them like you do, like in a museum."

I probably hit a raw nerve because it took about five seconds for him to respond. I actually looked at my phone to make sure I had not been disconnected. When he did I could tell from his tone that he probably thought I was a capitalist idiot. Whatever.

"So, you do know about an egg there." His tone was very cold and more of a statement than a question.

"No, sir, I do not. First of all, why would you think that? And, second, how do you know where I am?

"If you would like to discuss something computer or security related, I'd be happy to discuss that with you but, otherwise, I don't believe we have anything else to discuss." I paused, giving him an opportunity to have a change of heart and throw some money my way.

He chuckled, "Ms. Bell, you're in the computer security business, you know how easy it is to tag certain words on the internet. You also know how easy it is to find out where someone lives based on their liking something, like a picture of Chauncey Livingstone, on Facebook.

"Gracie Blanche liked the picture of the Fabergé Easter egg and then wrote, 'Cool huh Parker?' It doesn't take a genius to figure out you'd probably be going to Pothole sometime in the near future since you and Grace Blanche are friends."

He laughed and said, "I also pinged your phone and it triangulated where you probably are or have been."

Note to self, get someone in my office to fix my phone where that couldn't happen again.

He paused and then said, "Ms. Bell, I want that Fabergé Egg. You tell whoever has it that it is mine. I am willing to pay for it but it's mine and I want it." He hung up the phone. So much for détente between the East and the West.

I was still totally flummoxed on *why* he thought I had anything to do with the egg? Being friends with someone on Facebook does not constitute an actual knowledge of the whereabouts of this sacred egg.

Never let it be said that I am not a risk-taker. I dialed him right back.

"You have had a change of heart." No warmth there.

"I do not now have nor have I seen a Russian Easter Egg. Why you think I have this egg or know of its location is beyond me.

"Also, I would strongly encourage you to not to send your people to beat up women and put them in the hospital."

"You might not have it, but you know who does." He actually seemed to be surprised about the hospital reference. "What are you talking about?"

"Some Russians, rumored to be Spetsnaz beat up three women earlier today over your precious egg. All three are in critical condition in the hospital. Don't you think that was a bit of overkill?" I was fuming, and my voice was very clipped.

"Ms. Bell, I had nothing to do with that. I know nothing about that."

"Mr. Petrov, take this as a well-meaning warning. Do not do that again." I hung up the phone.

I called Missy and told her the entire conversation. "Get one of our guys to run the tapes on that call and see if they can detect any stress factors in his voice. I almost got the feeling he really didn't know anything about the girls getting beat up.

"Also, find out why my phone number can be pinged and my location can be found out. I thought my phone didn't have that capability."

Taking a deep breath, I asked, "Is, ah, Denny still around the Po Ho area?"

Denny Rowe, my former head security guy, and I had gotten into a bit of an argument awhile back and I had fired him. He and I both had had a bad hair day on the same day and our egos got in the way. Mine more than his. But I was right and I was the boss so I fired him.

He, Misty Dawn, and her husband John Boy apparently all took a liking to each other and I was guessing that he was still in the area hunting and fishing with them. Whether or not he'd come back to work with me was somewhat debatable. He had been black operations at one time for our government and I had a reasonable belief that he could easily handle a Russian Spetsnaz if need be. Plus, I knew that he could call upon specially trained security personnel to protect the Lady Gatorettes and Gracie Blanche.

"Maybe." Missy was somewhat guarded in her reply.

"Missy," I was grinding my teeth, "do you think he would come back and protect everyone?"

"Maybe."

"Aw, come on, Missy! Give me a break! Can you find him or not and can you find out if he'll come back?" My temper was starting to flare up. Well, who could blame me? It had been a stressful day. Plus, I was out of coffee. I couldn't even inhale a drop from the Styrofoam cup I'd been driving around with. I tried shaking out a drop but apparently the last drop had evaporated into the air.

"Give me a few minutes and I'll call you." She paused, "If he does come back, he's probably going to want an apology..."

"Not happening!" I snapped. I was still right, and I owned the company. Okay, maybe I was being a bit of a witch but...

"I'll call you back in a few minutes."

Bless her heart, in a good way. Southerners have at least one hundred sixty meanings of "bless your heart" depending upon the tonal inflection. She did call me back.

"Well, I do have good news for you." She was too perky. Not a good sign because this meant there was getting ready to be a negotiation and, as much as I hate to say it, Missy is a really good negotiator.

"Denny is still in the Po Ho area and he is willing to come back at our standard independent contractor rate and, yes, he's willing to get some of his guys down there within the next twelve hours."

"But. I feel a but coming on." I held my breath. "What's the bad news?"

"Well, he wants an airplane flown over Po Ho with a banner saying, 'Denny's the best' with your phone number."

"What?! Are you flipping crazy?! No, no, no! I flat out flipping won't do that!" I screamed.

Then, it was like a two by four hit me in the head. "Okay, you got me. What does he really want?"

Missy was giggling. "Had you going there for a minute, didn't I? Okay, what he really wants is for you to get John Boy a new John Deere tractor. Not a used one but a brand new one with air conditioning and heat in the cab and a CD player."

"Really? That's all?"

"Um, Parker, do you have any clue how much that's going to cost?"

"No, but as long as it doesn't cost as much as buying Disney World, I'm okay with it." I paused, "Oh, give him any color he wants."

Missy started to laugh, "Parker, they only come in green and yellow."

Yes, I knew that...maybe. What?! Do I look like I know farming equipment to you? Yeah, I thought not.

"Denny will come back at his regular pay but with the understanding that it has nothing to do with you but everything for Misty Dawn and the Lady Gatorettes."

"Really? He said that?" I was a wee bit miffed. I would have thought he might have missed me but apparently not. Could I honestly say I missed him? Um, not really. So, I guess we're really even then.

"Yes, he did say that, but I don't think he really meant it," said Missy. "I think he was just really burned out and needed a break. He may, and I emphasize the word may, have had a small touch of PTSD and the Po'thole area is a perfect place for him to decompress."

I couldn't disagree with her. I'm guessing special ops probably took a toll on the human psyche and Denny needed a little R&R. This area had great hunting and fishing. I was guessing that held a certain amount of appeal for him. Plus, his bonding with John Boy and Misty Dawn probably added to the natural allure here.

"I do think he's missed you, but he'll never admit to it...and you won't either." She laughed.

"Whatever," I grumped. "What does he think has happened to Misty Dawn?"

"He doesn't know because both he and John Boy have been trying to reach her. In fact, Denny said the locator on her belt isn't sending out any signals but John Boy's really not that concerned about it because he thinks she was messing around with it and probably broke it. They're both convinced she's out fishing by herself.

"I hope it was okay, but I told him about Anatoly Petrov and the Fabergé Easter Egg. He wanted to know what the big deal is about the egg. I told him we didn't know."

I love the way Missy said, "We don't know." Trust me when I say, her using the "we" word indicates she totally has my back and is making sure all sorts of security precautions are being utilized and put into place. In fact, I would strongly suspect she had already talked to Denny before I asked her to.

Since we don't normally deal with Russians in my company, individually or as a country, I feel comfortable in saying she had probably already amped up my personal security without me even knowing it.

"Parker, you still there?"

"Yeah, I was just thinking."

"You'll strain your brain if you do it for too long." Missy laughed.

I snorted, "Probably. Okay, I'll be back in a couple of hours and would you…"

"You'll have a hot meal waiting on you and your coffee stash has been replenished."

I sighed, "Missy, you'll make someone a wonderful wife one day."

"Parker, get on the road and get back to Po'thole."

Someone tapped on my window and caused me to scream. Potus let loose with his manic dog-barking, warning anyone who is even thinking about entering the party wagon that they were going to be severely maimed. Missy was still on the phone trying to make herself heard. It was a losing battle.

"Hold on!" I shouted at her.

I pushed the button on the window and let it down a little. There was a hideous dog-faced, flat-nosed, squinty-eyed, bald-headed man standing there with a gun pointed at me. He definitely was not local or state law enforcement. This guy looked like he'd slice and dice his mother-in-law for practice.

"Get out of that vehicle." He growled.

My brain went into overload, and not in a good way. My nasty, big-city ways kicked into gear.

"Why?"

"Because I said to."

I laughed, "That's not a good enough reason." I punched the button and the window rolled back up.

Would you believe that jerk fired his gun into my window? I was furious. A few choice words not heard in any sanctified church escaped my lips. The good news is the party wagon can take a bigger hit than that.

Missy was shouting in the phone. "Parker, Parker, what's happening?" And then her voice went into a totally calm 9-1-1 mode and said, "You have two approaching the back of the party wagon and one is standing at the door. They only have handguns and those won't penetrate the walls. I do suggest, however, that you get out of there as fast as you can."

"Like you didn't think I was in the process of doing that," I snarled. "By the way, can you rotate the cameras on top and see what kind of vehicle they're driving?"

There was no way the party wagon could outrun a fast car.

Potus was standing guard at the door and growling. All I had to do was say the word "cat" and he'd go through the door and kill whatever or whoever was out there.

Everyone seems to expect the word "kill" or the German word "toten" as the only words socially acceptable to be used against intruders. The word "cat," however, causes intruders' brains to go 'what?' and that's long enough to slow them down for just a second while Potus will make them wish they had never entered into a life of crime.

Before I start getting hate mail, let me re-assure you that cats were never used to train Potus. Keep in mind, any word would work. Why? Because animals don't speak English, they go by the sound of the word and base their actions on how they've been trained to respond to that sound.

Potus would definitely shred someone who was trying to enter into his domain, particularly if he had been told to guard that area...EXCEPT for the Lady Gatorettes. He loves them, particularly Misty Dawn. I have absolutely no clue why he's so drawn to her. While in some primordial way that made me jealous, it did provide a sense of comfort knowing that both of them would die in a valiant effort to save me. Let me hasten to add, I don't want either one of them to die.

"Parker, they're in a Mercedes and," slowly she said, "it looks like they have some type of diplomatic plates on the front of the car."

"What? You've got to be kidding me! In South Georgia, there's someone who has diplomatic plates on a car?" I snorted, "Let me guess it's Russian, right?"

I was really just making a joke as I mashed the gas pedal and left the gas station. I merged back on the interstate heading toward Florida. Unfortunately, diplomatic license plates could be purchased online and I had no way of knowing if they were legitimate or not. That guy, though, was so grisly looking an anteater wouldn't claim him as a kissing cousin.

Okay, so I'm a snob when it comes to male looks. I prefer guys who are at least five- foot eleven or taller and look like a ruggedly, handsome model. Realistically, I usually end up dating nice looking men but ones who will never grace the cover of GQ.

Is that superficial? Well, yes, and it probably explains why I'm still single. Also, I think it's a step in a twelve-step program somewhere for superficiality.

BUT, I can afford to be picky and, honestly, I've never seen myself as part of a Mr. and Mrs. combo package. I like being single. Dates are good but I'm just not into long-term relationships. I have the attention span of a gnat and the patience of someone who is undergoing dental surgery without Novocain. I've found very few men who can handle that combination. In short, I get bored easily.

"I can't tell on the diplomatic plates but they're hours away from Atlanta where, if they had offices, that's where they should probably be. Parker," she slowly said, "are you sure you don't know anything about the Fabergé Easter Egg?"

"No, a thousand times no." I gritted my teeth as I was looking in the mirrors to see if I was being followed. So far, I didn't see them but, then again, it's hard to outrun a cell phone call to someone ahead.

"I don't understand any of this. See if you can get hold of Anne and Chauncey and find out why people think *I'm* the one who knows something about this egg. Maybe they have a clue. Whatever is going on is just flat out weird."

"Okay, later then."

I was truly perplexed. This was starting to turn into something very twisted and convoluted. It was something I didn't want to be a part of.

CHAPTER 11

I pulled into the driveway of what used to be my childhood home. I'm not normally sentimental but after a rotten day of some whacko guy shooting a gun directly into my RV window, being nervous all the way back to Po'thole, finding out that my oldest friend Gracie Blanche was on life support and Myrtle Sue, and Flo had been beaten up and this was all over some silly Russian Easter egg. Well, it would have been nice to come back home where there had been some semblance of love still being harbored in the walls of a home.

Unfortunately, that was not to be. What was sitting in front of me was a building consisting of plastic and aluminum. Because my parents were now having fun in the big mansion in the sky and I had accidentally blown up the last living thing that reminded me of them, this new double-wide mobile home could not take their place. It was like a pretty hotel room, it looked nice, but you didn't really want to live there. This was a house and not a home.

I suddenly realized my condo in Atlanta was exactly like this modular home in Po'thole. It was functional but no real warmth and, much as I hated to admit it, no love. Both places were decorated nicely but it wasn't the same thing as walking into home and feeling the love.

Then it dawned on me. Other than people who worked for me at my company, I didn't have a single friend who I could really and truly call on in an emergency. Everyone I knew outside of work, which was only a handful of people, I did not even have their phone numbers. Oh, sure, I had tons of friends online, but could they help me out in an emergency? Um, not unless it was for something online. In the physical world, they would be of no help whatsoever.

Here, in Po'thole, I had the Lady Gatorettes and a handful of others I had known since I was in grade school. I was absolutely positive that if I called on any of them, they would come running to help me out.

My eyeballs started to sweat. Oh, mercy! What was happening to me?! Was this a hormonal attack? I quickly looked at the calendar on my cell phone. Nope, wasn't that.

Could it be, heck, my brain didn't even want to go to the next thought, but could it be that Po'thole might have some endearing qualities that I couldn't find in Atlanta? Something called friends, true friends, real friends, friends who would help you out at the drop of a hat simply because they had known you since they could spit in kindergarten? Okay, so maybe they weren't the most upscale people in the world...not even by Po'thole standards but they were the salt-of-the-earth folks who'd give you the shirt off their backs if they liked you.

Then I had an epiphany, a really scary one. Maybe I should move back here. After all, my work could be done from anywhere and I had the company set up to run pretty much without me doing much hands-on these days. It took me the same amount of time to go to the Jacksonville airport as did for me to go to Hartfield in Atlanta.

"Stop it!" I screamed. I didn't realize the words had entered into the world outside of my mouth until Potus growled menacingly and looked at me questioningly.

"It's okay, boy. The monkeys were chattering again and the words came out on their own," I said weakly. What was happening to me? Oh, my golly gee!

Pink's "So What" started playing on my cell. I quickly pulled myself together. It wouldn't do for a Lady Gatorette to hear me crying or even sniffling. There was a certain protocol to maintain around them.

"Hey, Rhonda Jean. Tell me the good news." I tried to sound cheery.

"Parker," she paused and sounded very depressed, "Parker, we still can't find Misty Dawn. Where are you?"

"I just pulled up in my driveway. Um, by any chance, are you in my house?"

"No, but I'll be there in five minutes." Click.

Pulling the phone away from my ear, I stuck my tongue out at it. Okay, so it's not a mature thing to do but so what. Climbing out of the party wagon, I carefully scouted the area to see if I could spot something out of place but, nope, nothing was out there. Potus ran up to the front door and was waiting for me to open it when it suddenly opened on its own...or so it appeared. Mary Jane popped up from behind the door. I almost screamed. Yes, my nerves were shot.

"I saw you pull up in the driveway," she explained. "I have supper waiting on you or do you call it dinner in Atlanta?"

Not wanting to argue about the finer nuances of what meals are called, I simply said, "Thank you. Rhonda Jean's on her way over."

"Yes, I know. I had to make double-sure I had enough for all five of us." She turned and walked back in my house.

Okay, there might a few things I don't do great, but I can add very well, and I can do it quickly. "Okay, there's you and me and Rhonda Jean. Who's the other two?"

"Denny and John Boy."

You could have waved a clove of garlic over me and I would have fallen over. I hadn't seen Denny in months and seeing him right now in the midst of my apparent relocation thinking wasn't really what I had in mind.

"They should be here shortly," shouted Mary Jane. "I have a cup of Australian Kangaroo for you. Missy said you'd probably need it when you got here."

I had halfway turned to look at the yard again but when she said cup of Australian Kangaroo my head whipped around like something out of the Blair Witch Project movie.

"Coffee," I breathed. "Coffee."

A cup was quickly thrust in my hands and the hot steaming liquid quickly disappeared down my throat. Mary Jane was a wonderful hostess because she immediately filled my cup again.

"Ahhh," I said contentedly after the second cup. "What's for supper? It smells beyond great."

"Anything would taste good after those cheap, nasty tacos you probably got at some gas station somewhere," she harrumphed.

"I swear," I snapped, "how do you know these things?"

She laughed, "Because I can smell your breath a mile away and Potus doesn't eat tacos."

We both laughed. Just then Denny and John Boy came in through the back door. Denny's eyes were scanning the room. He does that because it's saved his life on many occasions he claims. I can believe it.

I noticed they were both wearing Red Wing Classic Moc work boots and the boots were wet. They looked like they'd been standing in water.

Denny noticed me looking at the boots and said with a grin and a wink, "I can tell you're jealous already. I'll get you a pair."

I snorted and grinned, "Well, it does make a lovely fashion statement."

Just like that, we were both back in each other's good graces. We probably needed a break from each other and I'm guessing it had to do with the change of pace in this part of the country versus being in the South's biggest city. Decompression needs to be done slowly or you can get the bends. Apparently, he and I both got the bends on the same day from being submerged into a different type of craziness than we were used to. Whatever, it was good to be back together again.

Denny plopped down on the sofa and started untying his boot laces. Potus had his head on Denny's knee. John Boy sat down in the recliner, leaned back, and said loudly, "Hey, Mary Jane, get me a beer, would you?"

Mary Jane doesn't do well with orders and I never noticed that she had a particular fondness for John Boy so when she gave him the old stink eye look, I took a step back and protected my coffee cup by wrapping my hands around it.

"Do I look like your wife to you, John Boy?" Her tone could have frozen the Bering Sea. "Oh, that's right, Misty Dawn would NEVER get your beer for you...and I won't either. You want beer? Get your fanny up out of that recliner and waddle on over to the refrigerator and get it yourself!"

She turned back to stirring what appeared to be stew on the stove. I noticed she had a wooden spoon in her hand and her head was slightly cocked so she could see John Boy out of the corner of her eye.

John Boy sat there for a moment, grinned at me and Denny, got up, went to the refrigerator, and pulled out a Coors.

"I'm stressed, Mary Jane, about Misty Dawn. Cut me some slack, ya hear." He popped the top and guzzled half a can. Turning around, he reached back and opened the refrigerator door for another one before he plopped back down in the recliner.

"John Boy, don't you go drinking up all my beer," I laughed.

He grinned. "Nope, I won't. I'm only having two. We need to figure out what's happening here."

I quickly brought them up to speed on everything.

Missy called on my cell phone. "Okay, Parker."

"Yep, Denny and John Boy are already here and we're waiting on Rhonda Jean for supper."

She snickered. "Supper or dinner? I can't ever keep it straight when you're down there. You use them interchangeably. Okay, let me talk to Denny a moment, please."

I handed the phone over to him. Rhonda Jean was looking through the window next to the front door.

I opened the door for her and she entered slowly. She looked like she'd been crying...or she was so mad she couldn't see straight. It was hard to tell with the Lady Gatorettes.

"They won't let me see Myrtle Sue or Flo or even Gracie Blanche," sniffed Rhonda Jean. "I asked at the nurses' station what room they were in. They did tell me, but they wouldn't let me see them."

She wailed, "They don't even have security on their rooms. Whoever did this could come back and kill them!"

Well, unfortunately, she did have a point. I looked over at Denny as he hung up the phone.

"It's going to be expensive, Parker."

"Yeah, whatever. I've been blessed with a great company that makes a boatload of money and I can afford it. Put round-the-clock protection on all three of those girls." I did my version of stink eye, which had absolutely no effect on him I might add, and said, "Don't use some fat boy security company. I want people who will actually protect them if someone tries to do them anymore harm. This includes doctors and medical staff."

He grinned. "Whenever have I ever used a fat boy security company? Nope, I'll put some SEALs on these gals twenty-four seven. They'll be there," he looked at his watch, "within the hour."

I grinned, "You were already on it, weren't you?"

He nodded and winked.

"Okay, what's your take on this whole thing?"

"Wait!" shouted Rhonda Jean, who by now was sitting on the sofa. "Where is Misty Dawn?"

John Boy and Denny looked at each other and then Mary Jane and Rhonda looked at me.

"What? I have absolutely no clue about her." I was flummoxed. "Missy told me the signal on her belt was completely dead. That, right there, does not, repeat, does not make sense. Missy said that signal is supposed to stay alive through a nuclear war and it's dead now. What about you guys? Any clues?"

Turning to the guys, I said, "Missy said y'all weren't concerned about it."

"The last time we saw her was on the boat on the creek. She might not be answering because of the water commission boys," said John Boy.

He started to stand up to go get another beer. Mary Jane looked at him, slapped the wooden spoon in her hand twice, and shook her head no. He sat back down.

I looked at Denny and he shrugged. "I'm as perplexed about this as you are, Parker. None of this makes any sense. You said you and Gracie Blanche talked on the phone about this Fabergé Easter Egg and that was it except for her having a poster made up and showing to Anne and Chauncey. What do they have to do with the egg? How valuable is it, anyway?"

"Well, the answer to your last question is in terms of monetary worth, the egg isn't worth millions, but the historical significance is very high." I then explained the history of the Fabergé Eggs.

"Had you talked to this Anatoly Petrov before he called you?" Denny asked.

"Nope." I paused, thinking carefully. "No, not him personally. I've contacted his main company a couple of times for information on another project we were working on but never spoke to him personally. He is aware of us though. One of his people did reach out to us a couple years ago but it didn't go any further."

"What were they asking about?" asked John Boy.

I inwardly cringed. This was going into a highly confidential area and as goofy as I could be sometimes in my personal life, my business life was very, very precise. I specialized in a very narrow, and lucrative, niche of computer security. To put it bluntly, other than Denny, no one in this room was cleared for the answer to John Boy's question and I wasn't willing to give it up.

"John Boy, I work in computer security and that's all I can discuss. Now..."

He interrupted, "Parker, we're friends here. Why can't you tell us what those Rooskies wanted you to do for them?"

I looked John Boy in the eye and said slowly, "John Boy, I am not at liberty to discuss that. Let's move on, shall we?"

He thought for a moment and then nodded his head. If he tried to get the answer on any of my company's business later on from Denny, he'd find out that my comments were a virtual Chatty Cathy compared to Denny answering a question. He could google me until the cows came home and he would find out little to nothing about me in terms of what I did for a living. He could, however, find out tons of stuff on me about being a bestselling author.

"Hey, y'all, supper's ready. Let's eat." Mary Jane had spoken, and I was ravenous. I probably pushed everyone out of the way to get to the stew pot.

Say what you want about Mary Jane, but she was an outstanding cook. Beef stew, rice, fresh squash, and fresh broccoli with lemon butter and toasted sesame seeds was the best meal I'd had in forever. Okay, it was like twenty-four hours but whatever. I went back for seconds. Everyone was quiet as we chowed down on her meal.

Popping up from the table, yes, we ate at the dining room table for a change, Mary Jane went into the kitchen and came out with...banana pudding! Slap butter on my fanny and call me a biscuit! Banana pudding just caused me to go into ecstasy overload. The thought crossed my mind that maybe Mary Jane would be willing to make up different meals and put them in the freezer for me when I moved back here.

What! Oh, no! Was I really entertaining an errant thought that I might move back here?! Oh, mercy, I thought I could hear God snickering at me. Noooo! I was NOT coming back to this little dip doodle place! Surely God wouldn't send me back here...would He? Nooo!

"Mary Jane, that was a delightfully delicious meal. Thank you so much." Denny smiled and I thought Mary Jane was going to melt into the floor. She did look a wee bit flustered.

"Why, thank you, Denny. I appreciate that." She smiled so hard that a previously hidden dimple showed itself. I don't believe I had ever witnessed that before.

"Yep, that was good." John Boy belched, loudly.

We all turned to look at him.

"If you did that around Misty Dawn, she'd slap the squat out of you and send you back to your mama," snarled Rhonda Jean. "And I know your mama, she done raised you better'n than that. You apologize."

"Y'all ain't no fun," whined John Boy, "I get fussed at everything over here."

Denny laughed, "It's because you know better. It's one thing if we're out in the woods or on the river but you don't do that in front of ladies."

"They ain't...." and his sentence dwindled down to nothing as we gave him the death-to-the-devil stink eye. Then we all grinned.

"I don't believe I heard an apology for your lack of good manners," Mary Jane said sweetly as she slapped the wooden spoon in her hand, grinned, and had a diabolical look in her eye.

John Boy glared at her for a moment, ducked his head, and mumbled, "I'm sorry for burping. The meal was really good."

As everyone was nodding their heads in approval, my phone went off.

"Hey, Missy, what's up?"

"Parker, I have news on Misty Dawn," a slight pause. "It's not looking good."

My heart sank, not only for Misty Dawn and John Boy but for the sudden realization that I may be the new leader of the Lady Gatorettes.

"What is it, Missy?" I asked as everyone gathered around me.

"There's a very slight signal coming from the river and it appears that she's trying to send Morse code."

"The code signal isn't working?" I was perplexed. The high-tech location device Misty Dawn wore had a special emergency signal programmed in it. To be able to turn the signal device off and on to over-ride a constantly emitting signal was just beyond weird; but, then again, everything that was happening was weird.

"It's almost like there is a jamming signal that is interfering with the main one."

"Missy, are you sure of the location?" I was truly puzzled. "Could that signal be actually coming from somewhere else? Did you..."

"Yes, I've already called the manufacturer and they said no it's not supposed to do that. They said they had tested every possibility and what's happening with the device isn't something they can explain."

"However, the good news is they want to stay in touch with us on this."

I snorted, "Yeah, I'll bet they do. They don't want us blasting them to kingdom come on social media."

By this time, I was pacing around the dining area, living room, and kitchen. Even though I had Missy on speaker phone and everyone could hear what she was saying, they were still following me around. It was kind of like an adult version of ring-around-the-rosie game. Apparently, I have a lot more power than what I was giving myself credit for.

"Alright, give me the coordinates and let's go see what we can find."

I was grim. Denny was stone-faced, Mary Jane lifted up her shirt and made sure her hidden gun was still resting, I assume, comfortably on her hip. Rhonda Jean disappeared into the bedroom and came out wearing her orange-and-blue Gator shirt.

"If something has happened to Misty Dawn, I want her to see the Gator colors one last time," she sniffed.

John Boy was apparently so inspired by Rhonda Jean's devotion to Misty Dawn and the Gators that he whipped off his camo shirt. I was sure I was about to be blinded by pasty white skin. I was wrong.

Apparently, they ALL wear their beloved Gator shirts under their regular clothes. I was afraid to ask if they all had had their blood dyed orange-and-blue, but I wouldn't put it past them.

"Denny?" I cocked an eyebrow.

Grinning, he whipped off his camo shirt. Let me point out even though I'm not remotely interested in Denny as a romantic liaison, he does have a perfectly fine chest honed by many years of exercise that I have been privileged to see on occasion and which has caused me to have some very naughty dreams. He turned around and there on his left shoulder was a very tiny but visible Florida Gator tattoo.

Because Denny had been sent on many secret military missions in his prior life, ones that the United States government would disavow if he had ever been captured, I knew he didn't believe in having any identifying marks on his body. He wanted nothing that would indicate he was an American and causing more problems if he were taken prisoner.

The good news is that with his new tattoo that meant he wasn't going to be doing black ops any more. Or, if he did any more missions, he didn't care if they, whoever they were, knew he was an American and a Gator fan at that.

The bad news was he's been turned into an unofficial official member of the Lady Gatorettes. His loyalty to me was now somewhat suspect.

He must have picked up on my thoughts.

"No need to worry, Parker. I'm still yours," he grinned wickedly and winked. "I'm also a member of the club...as are you."

My heart skipped a beat. Did this mean I was going to have to get a tattoo? I love the Gators too and I am perfectly willing to wear orange-and-blue for the rest of my life. But, I'm scared to death of needles and while I periodically threaten to get a tattoo, I would never get one. What, and defile my perfectly good, pristine body? But noooo.

"Am I going to have to get a tattoo?" I nervously asked.

Mary Jane and Rhonda Jean started shaking their heads vigorously no.

"Yeah, I'm okay with everything," I said, looking at them. They high-fived each other. I wasn't sure what that meant, didn't want to ask, and instead started heading for the front door.

"Guys, you coming? We're wasting time here. If Misty Dawn is trying to signal us from the bottom of the river, we need to get our fannies in gear."

As we all piled in the party wagon along with Potus, Denny's phone rang.

"Yes?" Nodding his head a couple of times, he said, "Stay on it, repeat, stay on it. Defend and protect at all costs. Can they be moved? No? Okay, repeat, defend and protect at all costs. One in, one out, double up if necessary. Report via text every hour. Our language only."

We all looked at him with the oh-my-golly-what's-happened-now look.

He hung up. "Well, Gracie Blanche must have become conscious at some point because she bit someone who was apparently trying to smother her. My guy who was in the bathroom, came out, saw what was happening, spun the guy around, and was shot in the gut. He's in surgery now. Good news is my guy shot him in the head. Backup was there in just a few seconds and the girls are all protected. I had them double-up on the protection."

We all gasped, and I said weakly, "Way to go, Gracie Blanche, that's my girl. She's not gonna die."

Denny shook his head. "What is so all fired important about this Easter Egg?

CHAPTER 12

We were almost to the area where we could load the boat in the water when I spotted Anne and Chauncey walking. Things were just too odd about everything happening and maybe they could shed some light on it. By the way, it's not called kidnapping if they willingly get into a vehicle.

I pulled up next to them. "Hey, guys, hop in."

They looked at me quizzically. "Thank you, but we need to walk," said Anne, continuing to stride purposefully.

"Well, let me put it another way. You're in danger and I want to get you off the street before anything happens to you." I was firm. Denny was even firmer by jumping out of the party wagon and grabbing them by the elbow as Rhonda Jean and Mary Jane helped them up into the party wagon.

They looked a little befuddled at our actions. Then Chauncey asked, "Are you kidnapping us?"

Anne, the Tsarina, said, "Oh, my. Well, this will be a new adventure."

Denny answered for me. "No, not exactly. We actually are protecting you from some Russians who apparently think you have an original Fabergé Easter Egg and are willing to go to great lengths to get it."

Anne and Chauncey looked at each other, blank expressions on their face, and then Chauncey said, "What makes you think that?"

I snorted, "Well, Gracie Blanche, who was beaten up and is in the hospital now, said you have one of these eggs. Then I get a phone call from Anatoly Petrov, the Russian billionaire, asking about the egg. Next thing I find out is that Flo and Myrtle Sue have been beaten up and are also in the hospital. Misty Dawn is missing and, somehow, everything that is happening appears to be tied to this egg.

"What's really strange is that I'm somehow involved in all of this and I know nothing about it. Can you help me understand what's going on here?"

Chauncey had wiggled out of the backpack he always wore and had it sitting between his feet. Taking off his hat and smoothing his hair, then stroking his mustache for a moment, slowly asked, "Anatoly Petrov called you?"

I nodded.

Chauncey chuckled. "That's interesting."

"Why? Do you know him?" I asked. This was becoming curiouser and curiouser, as Alice in Wonderland would say.

"He's on the news a fair amount," answered Chauncey.

Anne was staring out the window, pretending to ignore what was going on, and then quietly said, "Where are you taking us?"

Mary Jane answered, "Misty Dawn has disappeared and we're getting a signal that's under the water near Grove Point Bay. There's an old road that goes out to it. We're trying to find her."

Anne and Chauncey exchanged a quick glance but said nothing.

"Mary Jane, where do I turn?" My GPS showed that I was supposed to turn into what looked like someone's driveway.

There was an old, caved-in looking home sitting to the right of the driveway. The front door was hanging on tentatively only by a hinge at the top of the frame. The yard was totally overgrown. It was pretty obvious no one lived there; however, I didn't like taking chances and having some looney toon run out from the bushes brandishing a shotgun or trying to impale themselves on the front of my vehicle. It wasn't on my preferred list of having things happen. Human beings don't clean off the front grill as quickly and easily as love-bugs do.

After all, this was Po'thole and you could never be sure what the natives might do. In my opinion, there seemed to be an unnaturally high population of folks whose cornbread didn't get cooked in the middle.

For those of you unfamiliar with that term, it means they ain't quite right...in the head...they're just one degree short of being committed somewhere, probably has something to do with multiple marriages and inbreeding. After all, this is a small town and the gene pool isn't that large.

"Go up the driveway and follow it to the river."

"Mary Jane, are you sure about this? It doesn't look right." I was still a wee bit nervous.

Rhonda Jean popped in with, "It's okay. This is the fastest way to Grove Point." Pausing, "Not many people know this way."

I rolled my eyes. "Anybody know who owns this property?"

Denny, John Boy, Rhonda Jean, and Mary Jane shouted at the same time, "You don't need to know that!"

Okay, then. I decided to concentrate on the overgrown, very rutted driveway. Tree branches were scraping across the top of the RV.

About four hundred yards from where I had turned into the driveway, there was the river. You definitely couldn't see it from the road. In fact, it appeared that the foliage had popped back into its natural position. It was a wonderful hiding place. Even though I had grown up in this area, I didn't have the slightest clue that any of this existed. It was, in its own way, breathtakingly beautiful.

The road ended right at the top of a small bluff overlooking the river. The river was sparkling as the sun's rays danced across the little waves. Old oak trees created a natural arbor canopy and, surprisingly, there weren't any mosquitoes. The trees had probably been around since before the Civil War. If they could talk, I'm sure the stories they could tell would be fascinating.

We all climbed out. Anne and Chauncey looked like little kids at Disney World seeing a new ride for the first time. Their eyes sparkled with delight at this new area they could hike and explore to their hearts content.

Mary Jane and Rhonda Jean disappeared to the left of the RV into what I thought was just wild azalea bushes. Apparently, there was a hidden path that you had to know about because you couldn't see it AND you had to push the bushes apart to get to it. Let me point out that you don't have to do these things in Atlanta.

"Wait!" shouted John Boy. "Let me see if there are any footprints."

He and Denny pushed the girls aside, they stopped once they got past the bushes, and squatted down, peering at the dirt in the path.

"Y'all stay up here," ordered Denny. "Parker, see if you can get the party wagon turned around. You should be able to do with Mary Jane and Rhonda Jean helping you out."

Since when did Denny use the word 'y'all'? I just nodded. The guys disappeared down the path. Anne and Chauncey had wandered over to an old concrete picnic table and sat down observing our actions. I got back in the RV and with quite a bit of maneuvering managed to get it turned around and heading back out the way we had come in.

I didn't say it out loud but when Denny said get it turned around, I knew we were either going to have to make a quick get-away or we'd have to take someone to the hospital...perhaps even the funeral parlor. Neither scenario was a good thing as far as I was concerned.

My cell phone twice vibrated in my back left jeans pocket, a small thrill but not enough to make me gleeful and dance. I pulled it out and looked at it.

"In ten, ready to go, door open. Repeat."

Okay, whatever they've found means life or death. I looked around to see where everyone was. The Tsar and Tsarina were still at the picnic table. I wondered vaguely why a concrete picnic table was here, but I didn't spend any length of time pondering that.

I waved for them to come back to the RV and also to Mary Jane and Rhonda Jean.

"Yeah, what's up?" asked Mary Jane, hustling over and climbing into the RV.

"Denny said to be ready to go in ten minutes and three of those minutes have been used up. When he says be ready to go, he means be in your seat and ready to go. No questions, no dawdling, just be ready to go."

Everyone climbed in, sat down, and, surprisingly, no one was talking. I did notice that Mary Jane had placed a towel on her lap and, being the bright astute person that I am, I surmised that she was holding her gun under it in case things went south.

My phone vibrated. It was a text from Missy. "Anatoly called and said you weren't answering him. I told him you were out of the area. He hung up."

I love emoji's, so I sent her back a thumbs up icon. I double-checked my phone for missed messages, didn't see any, and was just starting to wonder about Anatoly's alleged call when the phone vibrated again. "Countdown starts now."

I'm such a bad dog owner sometimes. I hadn't even noticed that Potus had gone with Denny until he bounced through the door.

John Boy held the door open as Denny came in with an unrecognizable something he was holding over his shoulder in a fireman's carry.

"Go, hospital!" He ordered.

Rhonda Jean and Mary Jane started to get up when Denny snapped, "Stay."

He edged his way back to the bed in the back of the RV and carefully placed his package on the bed. I had gotten a good whiff when he entered the RV and it was not a smell that would ever be considered for a celebrity's perfume line.

"John Boy?" asked Rhonda Jean in a small voice. He ignored her and went in the back. Meanwhile, I had gunned the party wagon and came barreling out of the driveway a lot faster than I had gone in and almost skidded out onto the main road.

A few minutes later we were in the River County Medical Center ER bay and medical personnel had taken Misty Dawn in. They immediately wheeled her down to the MRI/X-ray area.

Denny and John Boy were filthy and stank. This was not your normal I've-been-hunting-and-haven't-washed-all-weekend smell. This smelled like decay, death, and massive infection. Truly, what little of Misty Dawn I had seen, I would not have been able to identify her.

We were all standing in the middle of the ER. One of the nurses said, "There's too many of you in here. Leave except for him." She pointed at John Boy. "We need to get information from you."

John Boy looked like he'd been caught poaching red-handed by the game commission.

"Yeah, okay," he weakly muttered.

"Denny, you need to shower. I'll move the party wagon and you can shower in there. There's clean clothes in there for you and I'm thinking John Boy can fit into some of your clothes when he finishes answering questions."

I looked at him and he nodded.

"Let's go, guys."

Mary Jane popped up with, "I'll make the coffee."

Turning to me, "Is there any food in that thing?"

"Pretty sure Missy had it stocked before I left Atlanta."

Chauncey cleared his throat. "The Tsarina and I need to finish our walk."

I semi-glared at him, dumbfounded. "Really? You want to finish your walk?"

Anne, always so sweet, gently said, "Yes, Chauncey needs to finish his walk. So, we're going to leave you and maybe you could call me later with an update?"

Stunned, I just nodded. These people were seasoned or call them old, but they were from Maine and I guess that accounted for them leaving in the middle of this chaos...or maybe they'd just had all of the bonding they could stand with us. But, it being so crazy, those thoughts didn't stay long in my head.

The rest of us went out to the RV and I moved it into the parking lot. Denny took his turn in the shower. John Boy came in just as Denny stepped out of the shower and into the bedroom. John Boy went into the bathroom, opened the door a wee bit, and threw his clothes out on the floor.

Rhonda Jean asked, "Parker, you got any trash bags? These clothes ain't never going fit to be worn again."

I didn't have a clue and shrugged. Mary Jane dove under the kitchen sink, came up with two bags and handed them to Rhonda Jean.

"Yeah, they're past ripe."

Mary Jane got coffee going and soon had some delicious hamburgers and homemade french fries ready.

In a flash, I was chomping down on a hamburger that could rival anything at an upscale restaurant or maybe I was just really hungry. Regardless, it was delicious.

A few minutes later, John Boy re-appeared dressed in a tee shirt and jeans.

Rhonda Jean asked, "John Boy, what happened to Misty Dawn or can you tell?"

He cleared his throat, his eyes were a wee bit watery, and said, "She was lying in the mud and muck under the dock. There was an old rowboat on its side in the water and my..."

He choked up, paused, and then continued, "My sweet Misty Dawn was under the boat and she had pulled her head up on her hand on the boat so she could breathe. Her other hand was trying to push the emergency button on the emergency belt buckle."

Choking up again, he put his burger down. "She was so covered in filth that Denny and I couldn't tell what had happened to her."

Denny took over at that point. "We went to lift her up and discovered she had a chain wrapped around her ankle. It was connected to a big barrel."

"Yeah, Denny put something on the chain and it fell right off." John Boy added.

Rhonda Jean gasped, "A barrel? Oh, my golly!"

Denny's eyes had turned into slits. Shaking his head, he said, "That barrel was heavy, but Misty Dawn had somehow managed to hold onto it enough to keep it from sinking in the mud and drowning her. John Boy and I didn't have time to open it. We needed to get Misty Dawn out of the muck and to the ER."

John Boy nodded his head. "Whoever did this to her is dead meat."

While it wasn't politically correct to agree with him; fact is, whoever was trying to wipe out the Lady Gatorettes and Gracie Blanche had now earned the dubious dishonor of being first on all of our most hated list.

I don't dare verbalize what I thought should be done with these jerks but, suffice it to say, it was nothing nice. I was really sure my thoughts paled in comparison to what the remainder of the Lady Gatorettes were thinking.

Mary Jane stood up, "Alright, if everyone is finished eating, I'll clean up. Go check on Misty Dawn BUT one of y'all have to come back and get me. Go Gators!"

We all stood up, did the Gator Chomp, and then we all grinned at each other.

Marching into the ER, I'm sure we probably unnerved some of the nurses, but the good news was no one tried to stop us. I leaned over the counter and glared at the charge nurse.

"What's the status on Misty Dawn?"

She glanced at the computer and said, "Room six, Doctor Hood will be there in just a moment."

"Is she okay?" I held my breath but realized if something was really seriously wrong, Misty Dawn would have been life-lined to Gainesville or moved upstairs.

The nurse looked up and smiled slightly. "Yes, but she's not a happy camper and wants to go home."

Collectively, we all breathed a sigh of relief.

Walking into the so-called room, it was actually a curtained-off space with just her bed in it, Misty Dawn's face was sort of cleaned off, but she still had muck and mud on her even though she was wearing a hospital gown. I didn't see her clothes and suspected they had been removed by the Hazmat Team.

Her eyes, nose, and lips were swollen but her sense of humor was intact. After saying a couple of choice words that tele-evangelists would be praying over for the rest of their television lives, she weakly whispered, "Go Gators."

We all laughed.

"John Boy," she whispered.

If there was any doubt that he was her true soulmate, it was erased when he pushed us out of the way and leaned over the bed. Even though she had an IV stuck in her arm and had other various hospital things wrapped around her arms, he gently slid his arms under her shoulders and around her waist. He was whispering something in her ear as his cheek was resting against hers.

Dr. Hood came into the room, looked us over, and said, "There's really too many of you in here."

Ignoring the good doctor, Denny stepped over and leaned into his personal space. "So, when can she go home and what's wrong with her?"

The doctor looked at Denny for a moment, probably deciding it wasn't worth the trouble it was going to create if he insisted we follow the hospital's rules – that was a wise decision on his part. Just saying.

"She's very dehydrated but she should be fine in a day or two. Ideally, she should spend the night where we can keep her under observation."

"No."

We all grinned.

"Misty Dawn has spoken," said John Boy, his face still buried next to hers. "I'm taking her home and keeping watch over her. Give me an instruction sheet if it's something other than common sense."

Hood dropped his stern look and grinned, "I'm sure she'll be completely safe with you. Just make sure she drinks a lot of water and Gatorade..."

We all erupted with "Go Gators!"

He just shook his head and his grin got bigger. "No alcoholic beverages for a couple of days. Lots of rest. I did prescribe some antibiotics just for precaution because she had been in that water for a while and for all of the mosquito bites. I didn't find any snake bites though.

"She's incredibly lucky she's still alive. She's got an amazing will and determination to live. She does have severe arm strain from holding up the boat anchor and she's darn lucky she didn't drown." He looked at us sternly and said, "No more initiation rites, okay? Somebody could die."

Initiation rites? No telling what John Boy had told the hospital people. None of us dared to look at each other. We all knew what kept Misty Dawn alive was all of the plotting and planning she was doing in her head on how she was going to kill the unfortunate person or people who did this to her.

We also knew she and John Boy hadn't told the hospital staff exactly what had happened, and I would agree with that; otherwise, they would have called law enforcement and that was not what any of us wanted at the moment.

John Boy turned to the doctor. "Get whatever paperwork you need signed and then we're going home. By the way, do you like venison?"

I cringed, knowing that John Boy had probably field dressed it properly but that it was also probably shot and killed illegally. HOWEVER, that part wasn't my problem and I decided I didn't need to take ownership of that priceless bit of information.

The doctor blanched. Aha! I knew he wasn't a fan of deer meat.

"Um, no, thank you for offering." Turning, he said, "Staff will be in just a moment to take out..."

He stared, probably in horror, that Misty Dawn yanked the IV out of her arm without so much as a blink. I almost threw up watching her do this. Of course, it probably didn't help that the fluid was still dripping out of the needle when she pulled it out. I was trying to take deep breaths to avoid losing my lunch. I was probably the only one who had an adverse reaction watching her do this. No one else in our group even blinked so much as an eye witnessing this.

Of course not! They all run around out in the woods and see all sorts of strange stuff all the time. Me, I stay behind a computer a lot...except when I'm down here and I'm forced into activity that doesn't involve a computer.

Misty Dawn growled, "I'm going home now. Send the paperwork to my house. John Boy, help me up and get me outta here."

The doctor almost ran out of the room and within twenty seconds someone from administration was in the room thrusting paperwork at John Boy. He ignored the woman as Rhonda Jean reached for it, signed it, and handed it back to her. The poor woman had gone into shock, didn't ask how Rhonda Jean was authorized to sign for Misty Dawn, and backed out of the room with the newly signed paperwork. I was pretty sure Rhonda Jean knew how to sign Misty Dawn's signature perfectly.

Sensing my thoughts, Rhonda Jean grinned. "We know how to sign each of our names. It's part of being a Lady Gatorette. We protect each other."

I strongly suspected they probably also had a training camp they disappeared to once a year to go over possible situations like this.

Misty Dawn tried to smile. "Glad you guys are wearing God's colors."

In unison, we all chimed, "Go Gators!"

John Boy scooped up Misty Dawn in his arms like something you'd see in the "An Officer and A Gentleman" movie and walked through the ER doors. She was still wearing the hospital gown and John Boy had managed to keep it wrapped around her and not expose her flesh to potentially prying eyes. Rhonda Jean put a Gator tee shirt on Misty Dawn's stomach as they were exiting the ER. Gators forever!

Getting her in the party wagon was a piece of cake. Deciding where she needed to be taken turned into a free-for-all. John Boy wanted to take her home but apparently wasn't willing to wait on her hand and foot as she thought he might need to. He wanted to hunt down and kill whoever had left her to die.

Rhonda Jean and Mary Jane each wanted to take her to their homes and that turned into a screaming fit between the two of them. It crossed my mind that we might be taking the two of them back into the ER because the strong possibility of bloodshed was looming quite large.

And then, Denny, God bless his little pea-pickin' heart – that's a Southern euphemism with a minimum of one hundred sixty-one definitions ranging from 'you fool' to 'death becomes you and I hope you die slowly' – offered my place!!!

Fear, trepidation, and hate exploded in my brain.

"Say what?!" I screeched. Now, admittedly, I really and truly didn't actually mean for those words to burst forth into the atmosphere. And I really and truly didn't mean for them to sound like I didn't *want* Misty Dawn to recuperate at my place, I didn't, but I also didn't want it to *sound* that way either, but I had visions of *ALL* the Lady Gatorettes and their spouses moving in to live with me.

For a single person who has lived alone for years, this is equivalent to having terrifying outer space aliens invading my world of peace and quiet. Attributes that are not normally associated with Flo, Mary Jane, Myrtle Sue, Rhonda Jean, and Misty Dawn.

Denny ignored my outburst. "It makes perfect sense to have Misty Dawn rest up at Parker's place. Everyone is over there all the time anyway. We have a great security system rigged up. Plus, a whole 'nother module can be added with more bedrooms."

Good thing I wasn't driving yet because I slumped against the steering wheel wondering why did God hate me so much. What did I ever do to deserve this? Obviously, the penalty is high, very high, for leaving Po'thole and then coming back. I wanted to die.

Oh, I could sort of tolerate being back here but dormitory style living, with the Lady Gatorettes no less, would cause a complete, and possibly long term, meltdown.

"No."

Everyone turned to look at me. I wilted.

"No to everyone living at my house. Misty Dawn can stay but no other sleep-overs."

Had I not been in borderline shock at this nasty turn of events, I would have paid a lot more attention to them high fiving each other. A LOT more attention.

CHAPTER 13

"Y ou and that darn egg!" snapped Anne as she and Chauncey walked away from the hospital. "Tell me again what your reason was for even taking it out of storage?"

Chauncey, never one to be overly chatty, pondered the question for a couple of blocks as they walked. "I thought it would be nice to take it out and look at it. The historical significance of that particular Fabergé is phenomenal."

"Don't you think just looking at it would satisfy your longing to absorb history? Why you had to take it to the antique show and show it off is beyond me." Anne was definitely not placated with his answer.

Another couple of blocks were walked before Chauncey said anything. "It would have been okay except Emma took a picture of it..."

"And you were proudly posing next to it." Anne was still upset.

"I didn't want to be rude and say 'no' when she asked me to stand next to it. That would have involved another explanation...one I didn't want to get into."

"And you don't think having it posted on Facebook is going to involve an explanation to someone, somewhere? People are getting hurt because of that one picture. Chauncey Livingstone, I am not happy with you."

He mused, "I wonder why Anatoly Petrov has involved Parker and the other girls?"

They finished their walk home in silence.

CHAPTER 14

Denny cleared his throat. "While we're having this love fest out here, I need to go check on my men watching Gracie Blanche, Flo, and Myrtle Sue. Y'all do remember who they are, right?"

"I'm staying here with Misty Dawn," said John Boy.

"And I'm taking a shower while y'all go see them," announced Misty Dawn. Grinning wickedly, she said, "John Boy, I might need some help."

Oh, Lord, have mercy! I didn't even want to think about them doing the banana peel thing in my shower. The good news is my shower is so small one person can barely fit in there and it's next to impossible to have two people in there. Don't ask me how I know this.

"Let's go," said Rhonda Jean and we all trouped back into the hospital. Yes, we went through the waiting room area this time. The poor little girl who was working the desk, unbelievable but Po'thole still has candy stripers Atlanta does not, looked up and cringed when she saw our motley group.

Putting on her best smile while her left hand inched carefully across her desk to the security button.

"Hi, may I help you?"

"Room number for Gracie Blanche..."

"Oh, her room is 248."

"Why do you know that number without having to look it up on the computer?" queried Denny.

Her face quivered slightly. "Because I have a note here on the computer that says no one is supposed to go up to that room."

Glaring at her although his voice was gentle, Denny said, "And yet you told it to us right away. Now why is that?"

And that's when the alarm let loose with its ear-piercing siren. She pushed back from her desk like a rocket being blasted off from Cape Kennedy and started screaming, "Help! Help!"

I'd like to be able to tell you security guards magically appeared and everything returned to normal; however, this is Po'thole where crazy is the norm.

A little old bent-over janitor with a filthy mop the same height he was hobbled down the hallway shouting, "I'm coming, I'm coming!"

And that was it. No one else came running out to assist this poor little girl. No doctors, no nurses, no administrators – although I thought I heard an office door being slammed down the hallway. I couldn't be sure because my ears were being deafened by the siren.

Rhonda Jean ran around behind the desk and yanked out the security button wires. That immediately stopped the siren. Unfortunately, it did nothing to stop the little girl from continuing to scream 'help, help' at the top of her lungs.

I almost felt sorry for her because no one was coming to her aid. Denny had grabbed her by the arm and was trying to tell her that everything was going to be okay when Mary Jane stepped over to her, grabbed the front of her candy striper apron, slapped Denny's hand, and jerked her totally upright.

"Kid, get yourself together," she snarled. "Your mama and your daddy ain't here. Stop your caterwauling or I'm gonna slap you and give you something to cry about."

I had visions of multiple lawsuits dancing in my head and being on the national news, not in a good way. Weirdly enough, I guess the little girl was used to being spoken to like that, sad I might say, but she straightened up.

Sniffling a couple of times, she said, "The only reason why I gave you the room number for that patient was because I thought you were going to hurt me."

Denny snorted, "Really? Because I asked you a question?"

He was still shaking his head when the janitor finally arrived, hobbling all fifty feet to us. "I'm here now."

Attempting to thwart us, he tried unsuccessfully to sound somewhat authoritative by saying, "Y'all need to go on and leave this little girl alone."

We grinned and left. There was no one at the nurses' station when we got off the elevator. Denny, Rhonda Jean, and Mary Jane pulled out their concealed weapons. Me? I had the weapons that God had blessed me with – my fingers, hands, and my teeth. Yes, I have been known to bite people. Of course, I might have been five at the time but since I eat on a fairly regular basis so I knew my teeth worked just fine, thank you very much.

The doors to room 248 and 250 were closed and no guards were protecting the doors, at least from the outside.

Denny signaled one, two, three and burst through the door. He had dropped almost to his knees when he hit that door. Good thing too because he would have been popped in the head by silenced gunfire.

"Golf!" He shouted, then smiled and stood up. "Good going, guys."

The two security men nodded. "We heard the siren go off and didn't know if it was a distraction or if something had really happened. We knew we could secure the rooms better by being inside."

Denny nodded. "Anything going on?"

The bigger of the two men said, "Yes, sir, right before the siren went off three women started to come down the hallway. When the siren went off they looked at each other, went back over to the elevator, and then I heard the stairwell door opened and close. That's it."

Rhonda Jean, Mary Jane, Denny, and I all looked at each other. Something was definitely going on but what.

"What did these women look like?" asked Mary Jane.

"Ma'am, they were approximately five nine to five ten, athletic build, late twenties, early thirties, brown hair all pulled back in buns, Slavic looking, probably Russian."

What the fongoo was going on? Now, we've got women wishing to do harm to Gracie Blanche, Flo, and Myrtle Sue? I had absolutely no clue as to what was happening...and I was sure no one else in our group did either.

Poor Gracie Blanche looked beyond pitiful in that hospital bed. Her face was still swollen, black-and-blue, she had so many tubes coming out of her that she might have been mistaken for an adult test tube baby.

My heart ached. What was so important about a jeweled Russian egg that someone was willing to kill, maim and destroy another person's life? Gracie Blanche and I had had our disagreements over the years, but she was my oldest friend since fourth grade and I didn't want to see anything bad happen to her.

If I thought Gracie Blanche looked bad, she paled in comparison to what Flo and Myrtle Sue looked like. Literally within thirty-six hours they looked like they had each lost twenty pounds or more.

Neither one of these gals was big or overweight to begin with and losing that much weight made them look like corpses. Rhonda Jean was the only Lady Gatorette who consumed more than her fair share of doughnuts and had a little extra weight on her. She also liked to point out that she was big-boned and it just appeared that she had a few extra pounds to spare. I had better sense than to voice another opinion.

They were on oxygen and had a boatload of tubes coming out of them as well.

"Whoever did this is going to die," grimly announced Rhonda Jean.

CHAPTER 15

E ven though I was now in safely ensconced in my bedroom away from whatever mayhem was going on with Misty Dawn and her caretakers out in the rest of my house, I was pondering over all the things that were going on. Why was someone going after everyone around me? It just didn't make any sense. Why was someone, probably Anatoly Petrov, *not* going after Anne and Chauncey? After all, *they* were the ones who had this supposed Fabergé Easter Egg.

Then it dawned on me that Chauncey had never answered my question about why I was even involved in this whole thing. I needed to call him.

Just as I was trying to find my cell phone on the nightstand, it rang. I screamed. Okay, so my nerves were a wee bit shot and then the bedroom door burst open. Denny was standing there holding a gun. Well, he wasn't just standing there. He had crouched low when entering and swept the room quickly before finally looking me in the face.

Holstering his gun, face grim. "What, Parker, what?"

"The phone rang just as I went to pick it up and it startled me."

He cocked an eyebrow. "It just startled you?"

I nodded and kind of rolled my eyes upward.

He bit the inside of his lip, nodded his head, backed out of the room, shutting the door.

The phone had only rung one time and stopped. Caller ID only showed an international number, but it wasn't the same number as Petrov's.

I hit return call, not really sure I wanted to know who it was.

"Ya?"

"You called." My voice was flat.

Some voices in what sounded to be Russian but, then again, I'm not really an expert on languages. It could have been Tongian for all I knew.

Another voice came on the line. He spoke heavily accented English.

"What you want?"

"You called me."

"Wrong number."

He wasn't getting off this easy. My naturally assertive temperament started to show itself. Some people would call it aggressive but they're not my friends nor do they work for me, so what I do I care?

"Sorry, Charlie, wrong answer. Why did you call me?" I snapped.

"You wrong person. Bye."

Let me give him the benefit of the doubt. *Maybe* it was a wrong number but with all of the crazy stuff going on, but I highly doubted it.

The phone rang again, this time it was Missy.

"Parker..."

"Missy, do you know what time it is?" I pretended indignation.

She ignored me.

"Parker, I think you guys need to get out of there in the next thirty minutes. We're picking up what looks like incoming pings all over the place and that's not good."

I groaned. "Seriously?"

"Parker, get out. If you can get to Little Sister's Cove, I have a houseboat and captain waiting."

"Seriously? I'm going to go for another ride on the river?" I sputtered.

"Parker, listen, he's going to take you up in a creek where there's a heavy canopy of trees. It's going to be easier to camouflage you there for the time being. Get going now!"

Missy was not one to panic and I did notice her voice sounded a little stained.

"Oh, alright. We're going to have to move Misty Dawn again. I can't imagine she'll be very happy about it."

"Just do it!" Click.

Throwing on a tee shirt and jeans, I walked out in the living room, clapped my hands and said, "Guys, we need to evacuate now!"

Unlike most people who would ask a lot of questions and run around like chickens with their heads cut off, this group was like a well-oiled machine. John Boy grabbed his night vision binoculars. Of course, he would have some nearby. What illegal game poacher would ever be without them?

Denny grabbed his pair and dropped through the hidden door in the kitchen floor. Although I had been initially annoyed about having a trap door in the kitchen, it had saved all of our lives on a couple of different occasions.

Rhonda Jean and Mary Jane came out of the second bedroom with Misty Dawn propped up between them. Potus was standing guard at the front door. Hearing two thumps from under the floor, we all headed out the front door and into the white SUV that Denny had pulled around.

I looked at him. "Really? A white SUV?"

"Looks like everyone else's around here. We blend in."

We arrived at Little Sister's Cove Marina and, as promised by Missy, there was a houseboat with a captain. We loaded up everyone and put Misty Dawn in the only true bedroom on the boat.

It had been completely quiet on the road over to Little Sister's because everyone was keeping their eyeballs peeled for who knows what, but we were prepared. Guns, knives, probably some hand grenades, smoke bombs, and a couple of things I probably didn't want to know about. Who knows where they got them, and I sure wasn't going to ask. Really. If using any one of those items could save my life or any of my friends, do you really think I would *ask* where they got them? Nope, not in a million years.

Now that we were on the boat, the questions started pouring out. Before I could answer any of them, Mary Jane had thrust a cup of coffee into my hands.

"It was the best I could do," she said apologetically.

I sipped it. Okay, it definitely wasn't the best I had ever had but it definitely wasn't the worst either.

"Considering what we've all been through, it tastes great, Mary Jane. I appreciate it." I smiled. "Okay, here's the drill. Missy called and said the house was getting pinged like crazy and we needed to get out ASAP, which we did. I do not know anything more than that."

I turned to Denny. "You know anything?"

"My guys say everything is secure from their end. Parker, what is going on about this Easter egg? I still don't understand how you're involved in this."

"I don't know either, Denny, I don't know."

Pink's "So What" started playing on my phone.

Cutting right to the chase, Missy said, "I assume you're on the boat."

"Yes."

"Okay," she took a deep breath and said, "So on your new home, I think we need to go with concrete block with a lot of armor blocking window shutters. A mini-compound probably isn't a bad idea either."

My head was spinning. I hate Po'thole! Every time I come here something awful happens. Two houses have now been destroyed, one of which was my childhood home, people died, and there was a whole boatload of crazy that seemed to follow me everywhere I go in this little stinky town. Why, God, why?

"Wha...what?" I managed to stutter out.

"Parker," her tone became very soft, "I'm sorry but your home was hit with what appears to be RPGs. It's completely destroyed.

"However, on the bright side, all of you guys are safe and I can have your home re-built fairly quickly."

"Why? Why me?" I muttered as I sat down. "What is up with this Fabergé Easter Egg? I don't understand."

"I'm on it, Parker. I'll get back with you as soon as I have more information."

I was stunned.

Denny said, "Let me guess. Your house was blown up again."

I'm sure my eyes were vacant because all I could do was nod. I was numb. Taking a deep breath, I stood up.

"Okay, gang, here's what we're going to do."

CHAPTER 16

"Yes, Ms. Bell, are you now deciding to return my Easter egg to me?" The heavily accented voice was Anatoly Petrov's and I had called him.

Ignoring his comment, I said, "Why is this particular Fabergé so important to you, Anatoly?"

Okay, I'm bad, so shoot me. I deliberately mispronounced his name – Anna toly instead of Ah-na-toly. I did it to irritate him in general, but I wanted to see if he would tip his hand.

"Miss Bell..."

"Please, Anatoly, we've always called each other by our first names. Let's continue that tradition." We hadn't and I was trying to be sweet about using his first name. Well, I did smile when I said it and I hoped my smile would travel the thousands of miles through the phone connections and he would know I was being nice and sincere. Alas, it wasn't to be.

"Miss Bell, as I've explained to you before," he explained frostily, "all Fabergé eggs belong to the Russian people and should be displayed in Mother Russia. I have gone to considerable expense to bring the eggs back to us. Why do you have such a hard time understanding this? Is it because you Americans have so little regard for your history that you would wish to preserve it?"

Aha! Now I've hit upon a raw nerve. It was dawning on me that this whole thing had less to do with the egg but something to do about the actual history of the egg.

Let me see if I could find out what the real reason was behind this massive chase of the elusive egg.

"Anatoly, was your grandfather involved with this egg?" I was smirking into the phone. Unfortunately, that came through the phone and not the winning smile that I had so hoped would.

"I have explained everything I'm going to explain," he snapped. "It belongs to the Russian people, not some American!"

And that ended our conversation, not because of me hanging up the phone on him. No, it was because he hung up on the phone on me. I never had that happen in my professional life, but it seemed to happen with annoying frequency in my personal one.

Calling Missy, my brain was whirling around faster than a kid playing with a fidget-spinner.

"Hello, Parker, and please don't tell me the boat has been blown up." I detected a slight sarcasm with a dash of humor in her voice.

Ignoring her, I said, "See what you can find out on Anatoly's grandfather. It would have been during the Russian Revolution and Tsar Nicholas the first."

"You want me to find a connection between his grandfather and the egg?"

"Yes. This particular egg isn't about getting it back to the Russian people. There is a personal connection for Anatoly. If I know what it is, then maybe all of this craziness will stop." I was so pleased with myself for coming up with *the perfect* answer on this whole Fabergé egg thing.

And then there was Missy. "Maybe. But have you thought about it maybe opening up a whole new can of worms? Like perhaps there is a secret message in it and no one is supposed to know about it? Or, what if his grandfather actually stole the egg and the world finding out about that might cause undue embarrassment to a very successful Russian billionaire? Or..."

I was highly irritated at this point. "Yeah, well, maybe but whatever. Find out if there is a personal connection there."

CHAPTER 17

Despite all of the strange and crazy things that were happening in the world of Po'thole being on the houseboat was relaxing. We drifted under a canopy of trees that were probably over a hundred years old. Birds were singing, turtles were sunning themselves on half-submerged tree limbs, a few fish would periodically jump out of the water, and my little gang of happiness were sleeping wherever they had plopped down.

The captain appeared to be ex-military, something that was probably a good thing considering everything that had been going on. He was mid-fifties and had a very buff body; however, I was so emotionally and physically drained that I didn't entertain any somewhat naughty thoughts. I passed out on the sofa.

Hours later, I smelled food cooking. Despite the wonderful smells emanating from the galley, my ever-discerning nose detected the delicious aroma of coffee seeping forth between the fragrant molecules of food.

Surprisingly, it wasn't Mary Jane cooking the food. She was out cold, curled up, and sawing wood. And where was this delicate bit of femininity sleeping? On the floor behind the chair and by the galley, her back against the wall.

Denny was also on the floor on the other side of the living area. Rhonda Jean had stretched out between two chairs and appeared to be sleeping comfortably. At least, she and Denny weren't snoring.

I knew John Boy and Misty Dawn were in the bedroom.

Who was cooking? The captain.

"Did I wake you?" he grinned. I immediately noticed his blue eyes and the dimple in his chin.

I laughed. "I smelled the coffee."

He handed me a cup and offered me the spatula. "Would you like to cook?"

Unladylike for sure but I almost blew out a mouthful of coffee. Shaking my head 'no,' I said, "I have the culinary skills of a five-year-old child. Nope, I'm gonna take a pass. You seem to be doing a fine job."

I hadn't noticed Mary Jane had stopped snoring, so when she popped up with, "I'll do the cooking." I almost screamed...but that wouldn't be cool with the super nice-looking captain standing in front of me. Instead, I managed to blink my eyes a couple of times to control my nervous system from erupting into ear-shattering screams. Yes, my nerves were shot once again.

Denny and Rhonda Jean stretched and yawned themselves awake. John Boy poked his head out of the bedroom and signaled for two cups of coffee. Mary Jane happily indulged him and then he closed the door again.

We had almost finished breakfast, although it was now mid-afternoon, when my phone went off. I looked at caller ID and shrugged my shoulders, indicating I didn't recognize the number. Denny leaned over and snatched the phone out of my hand, walked over to the doorway and tossed it in the river.

I wailed, "What are you doing?! That's a brand-new phone."

"Someone is tracking you with it."

"No, that's a new non-trackable phone that Missy gave me right before I came down here." I snapped.

"Well, you said Anatoly Petrov pinged you on it and found you. So, how's that working for you?" He snapped. "It's got to go."

Turning to the captain, Denny said, "We need to re-locate asap. Go further up the creek."

"How far do you want me to go?"

"About a mile, and will we still have direct access to the St. Johns River?" asked Denny.

"Yes."

"We need to start trucking it now then."

"Denny, I need to get hold of Missy. How am I going to do that without my phone?"

He handed me his. "I know for a fact mine can't be traced."

I called Missy.

"Hey, Denny, you having fun down there?" I rolled my eyes at the perkiness of her tone. "It's me, Parker."

Laughing, she said, "So, are *you* having fun down there?

"Not particularly." I explained about my cell phone now being a member of the catfish and turtle swim team. She laughed.

"Are you one hundred percent sure my phone is secure?"

"Yes."

"Okay, then who was the last person who handled my phone before you? Who programmed it?"

There was a slight pause and she said, "I programmed it, but Andrew was the one who put all of the new security features on it."

Oh, great. Everyone's out to get me and I really don't know why.

"Who?" asked Denny, arching his eyebrows. I started to laugh because when he arches his brows he ends up looking like a surprised emoji...or a muppet who's wigged out on caffeine.

"Hold on, Missy." I quickly explained the thin thread of connection on all of these Russians.

He nodded. "Tell Missy you'll call her back in a minute."

I handed him the phone and he went up on the outside deck. A few minutes later he came back down and nodded at the captain. I shrugged my shoulders. He nodded twice. I waggled my head, rolled my eyes and then nodded yes. Rhonda Jean and Mary Jane were just watching us, glanced at each other, smiled, and then gave the thumbs up sign.

Hoping they really hadn't figured out mine and Denny's communication or if they had they'd go along with it, I took the phone from Denny and called Missy.

"Hey, Missy, it's me again." I laughed. "I need another phone. Oh, before I forget, Denny wants to know how your cat is doing and if you're keeping an eye on him so he doesn't escape again?"

I laughed again and turned to Denny. "She wants to know if it's Noah you're talking about or Aaron or both of them?"

The captain half turned around and said, "She gives her cats people names?"

Denny nodded. "She's a Christian and gets rescue animals. She wants them to have a better life, so she names them after people in the Bible."

He blinked his eyes a couple of times, nodded, and re-focused on driving the boat. We were moving along at a fairly fast speed for a houseboat this size.

So the cute captain was paying attention to our phone calls. Interesting. I knew he wasn't one of Denny's men because they would never dream of saying anything about anything if they weren't spoken to directly.

"Okay, Missy, I need that new phone to go to the Summer Boys Fish Camp. I also want a second one to be delivered there but put it in Denny's name just in case. We'll be there by ten in the morning. Super, thanks. Bye."

We had a plan and it was going to be interesting to see what happened next.

CHAPTER 18

We moored the houseboat in a little creek that couldn't be seen from the larger one. The good news is there was an opening so there weren't any overhanging trees and their lovely branches couldn't deposit unwanted wildlife on our top deck. This would be better known as no snakes might fall off the branches and onto the top deck where they might decide to explore the rest of the houseboat, probably scaring the only person on the boat who is deathly afraid of snakes...me.

Nothing happened during the night and we headed toward Summer Boys Fish Camp. About a mile from the camp, Denny informed the captain that he was taking over driving duties. The captain seemed to be a little reluctant to do this and he also seemed a wee bit nervous at the same time. I had noticed he kept glancing behind the boat periodically.

Denny had obviously picked up that something was off about the boat captain. I still thought he was cute with those dimples but just the way he moved around and interjected himself into our conversations made me a wee bit nervous. He was being paid to pilot our boat, not become a friend. He also asked a lot of questions which we all pretty much ignored or gave him some off-the-wall answer. Plus, he seemed to be texting quite a bit. We could do that, but *he* was supposed to be working.

Denny must have suspected that the captain had alternative plans for us. Missy had hired the only houseboat available right then and had not had time to vet the captain. I had texted her to do a background check on him but so far she had not come up with anything. That alone made me and Denny highly suspicious. We had agreed to play it by ear with him while being cautious.

Rhonda Jean, Mary Jane, John Boy, and myself were on the front deck but had the sliding glass door open so we could see and hear what was going on. I knew Denny could handle whatever the captain might decide to throw at him and, depending on what he did and how irritated he might make Denny, the captain might be experiencing life in the creek.

Misty Dawn made her grand entrance to the rest of the living world by sticking her head out of the main bedroom and said, "Guys, we've got company behind us. Three guys in scuba gear just plunked off a skiff."

Denny grinned. "Did they 'plunk off' on their own or did they have a little help?"

Oh, mercy! What had Misty Dawn done now? I hadn't heard any guns go off but considering these gals could be in the Navy SEALS with their swift, silent, and deadly attitude they might have some type of silent weapon of mass destruction at their fingertips that I didn't know about.

""Well, their boat may have sprung a leak...a big leak." She winked. "We're downwind from them and I heard some funny sounding foreign language, so I grabbed the binoculars and saw the skiff behind us. The guys had Slavic-looking faces. To me, that means they're probably Russian which means I think they might have been the ones who tried to drown me."

"You know what Russians look like?" I was somewhat incredulous that any of the Lady Gatorettes would know what a Russian looked like. I was pretty darn sure none lived in River County.

She snorted, "I've watched all of the James Bond movies. I know the villains look like Russians."

I shook my head.

"Rooskies!" snapped John Boy. "They are dead meat!"

Looking around, everyone had a grim face except the captain. His face had gone from a beautiful natural tan to the pasty white color of someone in an open casket at a funeral home viewing. He sure looked guilty about something.

I noticed him slowly moving his right hand up under his shirt while he was looking at the air horn can. He looked like he was calculating how fast he could get to both.

"You move that hand one more inch, you'll never watch another Gator game as long as you live." Rhonda Jean's voice was so cold she could have frozen ice icicles in July. She hadn't moved but was staring the captain in the eye.

While Rhonda Jean was the largest Lady Gatorette I had witnessed first-hand how fast she could move if there was a doughnut involved. I strongly suspected she could move even faster because her beloved leader had been left to die and now this captain was acting very strangely. If she suspected him of having a gun, which it sure seemed like she did, and he decided to pull it on us his life would not be worth a plug nickel to her.

I had no idea what her weapon of choice might be. A hardened doughnut or even a bagel could be considered a lethal weapon to be used as a nasty Frisbee toss. Alas, none were available.

What was wrong with me?! I was now thinking in terms of food...again. The Lady Gatorettes' thinking was rubbing off on me. Not good, not good!

"Where is the egg?" he snarled. He pulled his gun from under his shirt, pointed at it Rhonda Jean as he reached for the air horn. He pushed the button on it twice.

Those things are loud. I also no longer thought he was cute.

It was bad enough that he wanted the Fabergé egg, had a gun on us, and used the air horn but then he made the ultimate sin.

"Gators?" he snorted. "We, FSU, beat you last year 'cas you were so lousy. So, yeah, chomp, chomp..."

Rhonda Jean was so fast with the ninja death star I never saw her throw it. She hit him in the throat. He dropped like a rock. She walked over to him, kicked him once, and snarled, "Who's gator bait now?"

God, please remind me not to put the Seminoles and Gators together in the same sentence unless, of course, it's about the Gators beating the 'Noles.

"Rhonda Jean, I..."

"He was going to kill us. I had to do something." Rhonda Jean explained, frowning at me.

She probably thinks I'm a wimp, but I was concerned about possible murder charges being made against her. Well, she could always plead self-defense.

"I didn't know you knew how to throw a ninja star," I weakly replied.

"Yes, I do," she proudly said. "I watched YouTube videos on showing me how to get good at it. I practiced...a lot."

She smiled, "Guess I done good, huh?"

What do you say after that? In my case, nothing.

I was still in a state of shock as Denny and John Boy tossed the captain overboard.

Since I'm not as well versed in the laws of nature as all of them are, I was trying to be helpful when I made a suggestion to them. Note to self, don't do that again.

"Um, Denny, shouldn't his body be weighed down so it doesn't stay up on the surface?"

He shook his head 'no' and pointed. There, swimming up to partake of the new catch of the day, was mama gator and her two little ones. I swallowed and turned away.

Denny took charge. "This totally means we've been compromised. We suspected this. Let's move on to Plan B."

I dialed my office.

"Missy, I hate, hate, hate that new coffee!" I screeched into the phone and then hung up.

Rhonda Jean, Mary Jane, and John Boy looked at me like I had lost my mind. Misty Dawn had already retired back to the bedroom.

"Um, Parker, I can get you any flavor you want," timidly offered Mary Jane.

Denny and I started to laugh.

"It's code, guys. In case anyone was listening in or tapping the company phone they would just think I was off my rocker. Missy will call me in three minutes or less. She has to get to a secure office and then sweep it before she calls me."

The phone buzzed.

"Hey, whatcha got for me?" I listened intently for a few minutes and then handed the phone to Denny.

"Missy, I'm putting a tail on Andrew. I strongly suspect he's not using the phones or computers at work if he's up to something. Does he ever leave the office for breaks or whatever?"

Hanging up the phone and then dialing another number, Denny nodded his head at me. I had absolutely no clue what it meant; however, rather than acknowledge my stupidity, I gave him a slight nod and smile back.

He was speaking Farsi to someone. While I don't speak Farsi, I do know what it sounds like. Heck, speaking formal English can be a bit of a stretch for me sometimes, much less learning to speak another language.

"Okay." Denny was all business. "Andrew takes a break about every hour and a half to go walk around in the courtyard. He takes lunch at exactly eleven thirty every day. No one seems to know very much about what he does after work.

"One of my guys is bugging his apartment. Andrew's car is going to have a flat and a kind-hearted tow truck person is going to help him change the tire while planting a bug on the car."

"Um."

"The tow truck person is already going to be out there fixing Missy's flat tire and will just happen to see this guy in distress, Parker." Denny grinned. "It's covered, he won't suspect a thing."

John Boy asked, "Are y'all gonna track him in real time or on a delay?"

"Real time."

I interrupted what appeared to be the beginning of a male bonding ritual over the use of technology. "Denny, are you and John Boy getting off now and heading up to Summer Boys Fish Camp or are all of us driving up in the boat and letting ourselves be captured?"

Honestly, it grated on my nerves to think I was going to let a bunch of men kidnap us when I had half of the Lady Gatorettes plus John Boy and Denny who could probably annihilate an entire army of zombies without even trying. BUT, and that was a big but, if it helped me to find out who was behind all of this craziness, then it would be worth it.

Denny grinned, "Oh, I think it would be fun to have you and the girls go right up to the dock and disembark. I think you guys should be laughing and carrying on the way you normally do."

Mary Jane, Rhonda Jean, and I looked at each other and started to grin when Misty Dawn popped her head out of the bedroom and said, "Party? Did I hear we've having a party? I'm invited, right?"

Everyone clapped and laughed. Yay! Misty Dawn was back in the saddle again and taking charge. While I enjoyed being in charge of almost everything else, being in charge of the Lady Gatorettes was not something I wanted to continue to do but I did one hundred percent want them on my side. It's called my safety and well-being.

John Boy asked, "Um, are you sure you're up to this?"

Aaand the stink eye appeared. I started to laugh...alone...at first and then the other Lady Gatorettes joined in.

Misty Dawn finally broke a grin and winked. "Oh, yeah, I'm ready."

CHAPTER 19

E asing our way up to the Summer Boys Fish Camp dock, we looked like a bunch of fumbling bumbling idiots which was our plan. We suspected we were being set up and if this was any group of men who didn't know who we were, then they were going to be in for a rude awakening.

After getting the boat moored - yes, I finally learned some boating words, we stumbled our way up the dock to the fish camp's little store, better known as a plywood shack with a couple of openings posing as the outdoor version of windows.

A tall guy with a face only a mother could love – a crooked nose that didn't look like it would ever be straight again, one unibrow going from one side of his head to the other, and a scar that ran from his left eye to the middle of his ear - came out just as we walked up to the door. He was wearing a black tee shirt with the arms cut out and beige cargo shorts with yellow flip-flops. I could just see him modeling this lovely fashion statement during New York's Runway week.

"What cho want?" he demanded.

"Do what?" I asked. I had my hands in my pockets trying to look nonchalant. I did take note that all of the Lady Gatorettes were slightly behind me and standing a few feet apart from each other. I prayed that if something happened requiring the use of force that Rhonda Jean wouldn't accidently hit me in the back of my head with her ninja death star. I had no clue what Mary Jane and Misty Dawn were carrying other than their deathly legal fingers, hands, toes, and feet.

Ignoring my question, he walked another couple of feet toward me.

"You Parker Bell?"

"Yes, why?" I tried to look confused.

"You waiting for this?" He held up a smashed stat phone and grinned. "It got hurt in mail when it delivered. You no call anybody now."

Bad news was it was playing out like we had all suspected.

I smirked. "Tell Anatoly he doesn't scare me."

He looked surprised. "Anatoly who? He no send us."

I was surprised because I thought for sure Anatoly was behind all of this. Cough, cough, who else could it be?

"Who did then?" I knew I was probably never going to get the right answer. Well, without some type of physical encouragement anyway.

"I WANT EGG NOW!" He shouted, his face erupting into even more ugliness. You know the old saying 'beauty is only skin deep but ugly goes clear to the bone'? His kind of ugly went clear through the bone.

Three other men stepped out of the shack. Unfortunately, the first guy was the best looking one of the group. These guys looked like rejects from some Dr. Frankenstein school of beauty. They all had multiple scars across their faces and whoever stitched them up, if indeed they ever had seen a doctor, did a really poor job on them. These guys were scary looking.

One guy was wiping a boning knife on his trousers when he came out. Unfortunately, I surmised the owner was probably dead. What was worse was that he had probably died over something he didn't know anything about and couldn't have possibly given the Russians any information whatsoever.

"What part of Mother Russia are you from?" asked Mary Jane, smiling. "I know some excellent chefs from St. Petersburg."

The guy with the boning knife waved it at her. "You no talk."

Misty Dawn snorted. "I thought all Russians spoke excellent English. You guys must have been born in the country."

"Shut up!" shouted the first Russian. "We want egg."

He started to reach under his shirt, for a gun I presumed. He was stupid and about to earn the wrath of three seriously annoyed hormonal women. I knew for a fact that none of them had eaten a doughnut in twenty-four hours and the lack of sugar in their bodies was probably going to cause some type of out-of-this-world crazy to erupt.

"Don't even think about it." Misty Dawn's voice was ice cold. Her hands were by her side. "Parker, back up behind Rhonda Jean."

I did as I was told. I didn't want to be hit by friendly fire and I was scared enough as it was.

The three Russian guys were talking to each other. The leader in front got a silly grin on his face.

"We going to have party with each of you. You no good, you die." He laughed.

"Who sent you?" Misty Dawn was as serious as I had ever seen her.

"Not this Anatoly. Me no know him."

"Doughnuts!"

Sure enough, there were doughnuts on the window ledge. I hadn't noticed them before but, then again, I'm not a Lady Gatorette who considers that a major food group and must be consumed on a daily basis.

Misty Dawn's hand was a blur, I heard a pistol crack, then the Russian screamed and grabbed his knee as it started spurting blood. He sank to the ground. The other three reached for their guns.

But now Rhonda Jean had a goal in mind. Those doughnuts were to be hers...at all costs. She shot both of the Russians on her left and Mary Jane shot the guy on the right.

Good news was the gals had shot each of them in the knee. These boys would never walk without a limp ever again. They'd probably feel really miserable in the wintertime in Siberia. Oh, wait, Siberia IS wintertime, all the time.

The girls snatched up the fallen guns as they were competing against each to see who could get to the doughnuts first. Rhonda Jean won.

Misty Dawn stood over the leader. "I'm going to shoot each toe off one at a time until you tell me who sent you."

"I'm Spetsnaz. I not ever talk." He managed to spit out.

"Not true." Misty Dawn picked up the boning knife, slit the guy's shirt open under his arm. "See? You're not even tattooed. So, no, you're not a Spetsnaz, not even close."

"You lied." She shot him in the other knee. He was screaming like a monkey in South America. "You going to tell me or what?"

"Misty Dawn. Stop." Denny had suddenly shown up. "I have a better idea."

CHAPTER 20

D enny had found his new phone in the camp's mailbox Missy had mailed to us. While the Russian guys had smashed mine, they apparently didn't realize the other packaged one was related to me since it had Denny's name on it. Plus, Missy had used a different return address on the package.

I called Missy to let her know mine had been destroyed but Denny's was okay. Apparently, everything at my company was going along smoothly. Somewhat annoying that my team did not need me but satisfying from the standpoint that I had set up the company properly so they wouldn't need me on a constant basis.

"Here's your phone," said Denny, leaning over the leader who was a ghastly shade of pale and alternating between holding one knee and the other one. He had pulled it out of the guy's shirt pocket.

"Call your boss and tell him that four women took you down. You've lost them and have no clue where they are and where they're going."

"Never." The Russian managed to say between clenched teeth.

"Do it. Just so you know, I speak Russian and can understand absolutely everything you're saying."

Another hidden skill of Denny's I didn't know about. Of course, he might have been bluffing but I sure wasn't going to call him out on it.

The guy shook his head 'no' and Denny promptly stuck his finger in the open knee wound. He screamed.

"Now," said Denny conversationally, "Are you going to make that call or not?"

The guy nodded. So much for being a Spetsnaz. Misty Dawn turned to Mary Jane and Rhonda Jean with a stern look on her face. "I hope you two don't fold that fast or that easily."

Not blinking an eye, they both nodded yes. Me? Heck, I would have given them the keys to my company had I been shot. I'd give them anything they asked for.

However, I never wanted to be the position to ever find out the level of my courage. It probably hovered around a one on a ten-point scale. I didn't want to explore that part of my psyche.

The Russian made the call. Denny had put it on speaker so everyone could hear what was being said. Denny was standing right there next to him with a faraway look in his eyes. I knew that meant Denny was processing everything that was being said.

By the end of the call, the Russian was alternating from borderline hissing to screaming into the phone. Denny suddenly leaned over, snatched the phone from the Russian's hand, and clicked the off button.

The Russian's eyes looked like Bambi in the headlights. "You get me killed!"

"Nope," said Denny. "I just saved your life. That guy will think you're stupid and a coward, but he won't ever use you again. So, you'll live another day."

Grinning, he said, "You boys need to find another line of work."

"You not leave me, us, here."

"Yep, that's exactly what we're going to do. Call 9-1-1 and they'll send someone out for you but we're going to be long gone by then and," he paused for dramatic effect. "You don't know how this happened and if you're smart, you won't give our descriptions."

Denny nodded to us. "Come on, ladies, let's go."

We all got back on the boat and were just about ready to push off when John Boy came huffing down the dock shouting, "Don't leave me! Don't leave me!"

Truthfully, I had almost forgotten about him.

"About time you showed up," groused Misty Dawn. "We were going to leave your sorry fanny here. Where have you been anyway?"

He jumped on board, the boat dipped considerably and then sprang back up to the proper water level. "I was going through all their stuff while y'all were keeping them entertained."

Hitching up his camo pants and spitting out a dip over the side of the boat, John Boy said, "Them boys don't carry a lot of cash with them. I only found three thousand dollars in the duffel bag in their truck."

Looking disappointed, he continued. "They don't have any good guns either. Nothing worth keeping."

Misty Dawn stuck her hand out. "Give it 'cas I know you're going to go buy more guns or knives and you've got enough of each."

"Aw, come on, Misty Dawn! You know..."

"How many chickens you plan on eating this month, John Boy?"

He handed over the money. When Misty Dawn got mad she was prone to going out to their chicken house and then they would be eating chicken in every form possible for a month. John Boy had learned his lesson the hard way several years ago and apparently did not want to repeat it again.

My cell phone rang. Although the number didn't look familiar, I decided to answer it anyway.

"Hello."

"Hi, Parker, it's Anne. I was calling to see if you wanted to have lunch today."

I didn't really remember giving Anne and Chauncey my cell phone number but then again I might have. There was just so much stuff happening that things routinely flitted their way into, through, and out of my head.

"Wish I could, Anne, but I'm out of pocket today."

"Okay, maybe another time."

Denny looked at me quizzically. "Lunch?"

"Well, since we're out here on the water and miles away from town, what did you expect me to say?" I snapped.

"Don't you find it interesting that they contacted you after we just left the Russians?"

"No, not particularly," I answered. "Although I don't remember giving them my cell phone number, it's totally possible I did. Perhaps for them to call me for lunch."

"Something's not adding up with those two."

"Denny, look at them. What do you think they're going to do?"

Why do I always think nothing's ever going to happen? I must have a dumb gene running around loose in my brain.

CHAPTER 21

"Do you think she suspects anything?" asked Anne, sipping a cup of tea.

Chauncey shook his head no. "She's going to attribute our having her cell phone number to that she simply forgot that she gave it to us. After all, she's been very busy."

He chuckled, never lifting his eyes from his iPad. "She's not the one we have to worry about. It's Denny."

Anne put her cup down. "Oh, I disagree. I think it's that group of crazy women. They're not as dumb or as flakey as they seem to want everyone to believe. Yes, they are rednecks, but they are smart. Had this been another time and another place, I do believe we could have turned them. They'd make outstanding operatives."

Chauncey snorted, "Not in Po'thole!"

Anne laughed, "True, unless there were a need for a resistance group. In a larger city, though, they'd do very well."

They shared the smile that only couples who have been together a long time know and understand. The smile transitioned miles and time.

A slight nod from Chauncey. "It's time to continue on."

CHAPTER 22

R honda Jean and Mary Jane had apparently expended so much energy on taking care of business with the Russians that they were in dire need of caffeine and sugar.

We misappropriated the Russians truck, stealing is such an unbecoming word to use, and found a convenience store. By the time Rhonda Jean and Mary Jane made their way to the cashier, they had cleaned out the store of all the doughnuts and all the brewed coffee.

The cashier had apparently seen way too many unfortunate individuals who had developed unnatural sugar cravings at all hours of the day and night. With a knowing smile, she commented, "Got the munchies, huh?"

Misty Dawn gave her a wicked grin, wiggled her eyebrows, and said, "Yep, we killed a couple of fellas this morning and it makes a gal hungry."

That kind of curbed any additional conversation with the cashier. As Denny pointed out as we were driving back to my place, that type of comment makes one memorable...

not necessarily a good thing if law enforcement came around and started asking questions.

Misty Dawn laughed. "She's not going to say anything to anybody about nothin'. You gotta remember, we're way out in the middle of nowhere. She's seen too much and knows too much about too many people. She's not going to risk her job. It's probably the only one she could get, and she needs it."

You can't argue with sound logic. Also, chances are, she probably already knew Misty Dawn and the Lady Gatorettes or of their reputation. It was wise on her part not to continue the conversation.

We had to stop at the doughnut shop in town before we reached my house. The gals had not consumed enough caffeine and sugar.

We pulled up into what was left of my house. Yes, Missy was right, it had been blown up to smithereens. We had to go back to the marina to get the party wagon. Until Missy got a mobile home for me, I'd be living in the party wagon. We had just parked in the front yard, or what was left of it, and relaxing, although it occurred to me this must be what it's like having small children running around loose all the time. A mother I did not want to be.

And then my phone rang. "Hello."

"Why you do that to my guys?" No accent but not proper English either.

"Do what?" I was wavering my hand at Denny and pointing at the phone.

"You hear me. No speaker phone."

"You know what? You guys are bugging me." I snapped, "Why don't you tell me what's going on?"

"You already told. We want Fabergé egg. You have it. We want it back."

Now I was totally perplexed. Why did everyone think I had the egg? I hadn't even seen it!

"Okay, listen up. I do not have the egg, I don't know who has it. I don't even know if it's real, and I've never even seen it. Leave me alone!"

"We know you have it. Short lady says you have it."

Oh, no! Did Gracie Blanche give these crazies my name when she was being beaten up? Probably, in an effort to save her life. If that was the case, I couldn't blame her. I would probably do the same if I were in the same situation. She knew I had Denny and the Lady Gatorettes to protect me; however, it royally ticked me off to think she would throw me to the wolves. I didn't think she would really do that but one could never be sure.

Yeah, convoluted thinking for sure. My therapist was going to have a field day with this upon my return to Atlanta. Yes, I have a therapist because my executive insurance coverage requires I see someone twice a year whether I want to or not. Mostly I spend that time sleeping on her couch and not talking.

I was seething. "You put Gracie Blanche, Flo, and Myrtle Sue in the hospital over some stupid egg?"

"You no understand." His voice was flat.

Denny indicated to me to tell the guy to hold on.

"Hold on." Ice cubes could have been frozen as cold as my words were.

Turning to Denny, I said, "What?"

"Tell them you have the egg, you'll give it to them tomorrow, and have them meet you at the airport."

"Say what! Are you flipping nuts?" I shouted at him.

Denny rolled his eyes. "Just do it, Parker. I've got a plan."

Glaring at him, I turned back to the phone and said, "Alright. You win. I'll have the egg at the airport tomorrow at ten. I'll meet you on the tarmac."

"Airport? Minute." He came back on in less than a minute. "You bring egg to airplane, you leave."

"Yeah, yeah, okay. Tomorrow morning at ten. Don't be late." I clicked the off button and threw my phone across the room. So much for staying calm during trials and tribulations.

Turning to Denny, I started to open my mouth when Misty Dawn said, "Parker, you stress about the littlest stuff. Mary Jane's pretty good with crafty stuff, we have the internet and we can find out what the egg looks. Mary Jane can whip something together, we'll put it in a box and you can give it to them in the morning. Easy peasey!"

The remaining Lady Gatorettes were looking pleased as punch at their solution.

"Of course, it would be better if Myrtle Sue made it. She's a little bit more crafty than I am," said Mary Jane. "But she's still in the hospital."

"You'll do fine," encouraged Rhonda Jean. "They won't know it's not the real thing until they go boom."

"Do what?" I eyed them suspiciously. Obviously, they were busy making plans while I was on the phone.

"Me and Denny are going to blow them Rooskies out of the air," proudly said John Boy.

Ignoring me, Denny said, "We've all got our parts to do. Let's get on it."

After they left, it was just me and Denny eyeing each other.

"Blow up an airplane, Denny? Seriously, since I'm the last person to see them, I'm going to be blamed for this.

"In case you haven't noticed, I'm not real fond of going to jail or trying to hide from law enforcement."

He started to laugh. "Really, Parker? You think I'm going to let you take the blame for that? Here's what's going to happen."

CHAPTER 23

"So why do you want John Boy to think that we're going to blow up the plane?" I asked. I was still very suspicious that somehow I was going to be blamed for anything that might happen to the Russians.

"These guys aren't the brightest bulbs in the box," said Denny. "I think they stumbled onto something and decided to take advantage of it. It's kind of like Dumb and Dumber but Russian style.

"All I'm going to do is plant a bug in the box and in the egg. Hopefully, we'll be able to find out who's behind them and what they're hoping to gain out of it."

"Well, that does make sense," I agreed. "But why tell John Boy something different?"

Denny laughed. "Because I don't want him helping on this. He really would get us all thrown in jail."

I could understand that. "Are we going to be using Andrew to do the translation?"

He grinned. "Not a bad idea, Parker. We'll have him do it from your end and I'll get Vasily from my end."

"You're not going to do it?"

"Nah, I need to check on several other things at the same time and I'd rather Vasily do it."

I'd met Vasily several years ago and he was cute. Tall, slender, looked Greek with smoldering black eyes and dark hair, with the charm and manners of an old-world European gentleman. Apparently, I must have started drooling because Denny started to laugh.

"Seriously, Parker! He has that effect on you?" he laughed. "I need to have him around more often."

He winked at me. "Remember, no messing with the hired help."

He winked again. "Per our agreement years ago."

Grrrr! How could I forget? When I first hired Denny and his company, there was a Sandra Bullock look-alike gal who was working for my company. Denny took one look at her, promptly fell in love – well, as much love as a former black ops guy could muster up – and told me he was going to ask her out.

I said no along with the totally inappropriate comment of "you don't get your meat where you get your honey."

Now I could be sued for that type of comment; however, good sport that Denny was, and how much money I was paying him, he decided to forego the "love of his life" as he put it.

Yes, she still works for my company. Yes, she's totally aware of the effect she has on Denny. Yes, she flirts with him every time he comes into my office. And, no, she is not remotely interested in him. She's in a committed relationship with her partner of ten years.

I hate it when he reminds me of something that I instigated. Alas, Vasily was making my heart go pitty-pat. I wondered if I could get Denny to fire him.

"Um, Denny."

"No, Parker, I see that look in your eye." He was laughing, "I'm not going to terminate him for a couple of days or weeks just so you can turn him into your boy toy."

"Whaa? I didn't say anything!" I retorted.

"You didn't have to. I saw that look in your eye."

We both started laughing.

"It's a shame we know each other so darn well," I finally managed to sputter out.

"True dat!"

"Oh, mercy! Denny, you're starting to talk like the Lady Gatorettes!" Still laughing, I added, "That's not necessarily a good thing."

"Dat's right!"

We were both laughing so hard neither one of us heard the light tap at the door. Then a more insistent knock.

I was still laughing as I opened the door.

There stood Bill Webble, my older next-door neighbor. He was tottery on a good day and he was barely able to stand at my RV door. He was a wee bit pale looking and in a milli-second my brain wondered if he was going to drop dead on my front doorstep. That was an experience I did not want to have.

"Parker, you should know," he wheezed out, "your picture is on the tv news that you killed a bunch of people. You're wanted and considered armed and dangerous."

Well, that shocking bit of news just killed my laugh party. Not to mention, I was stunned.

"Do what, Bill?" I paused, trying to figure out what was going on. "I'm on the news for killing some people? Who are they? I mean, who did I kill?"

He actually had tears in his eyes. "You killed your friends in the hospital when all they were trying to do was be friends with you.

"Parker, how could you do this? Your mom and dad would not be happy about this."

Denny slid out in front of me, out the door, and shut it. What was happening? I was stunned. Gracie Blanche, Mary Jane, and Flo dead? The tears welled up and made a mad dash down my cheeks. I turned and sat down on the sofa.

My mind was in a freefall spin. If I lived anywhere else but Po'thole, I'd be arrested for being a suspected serial murderer. There was just way too much craziness going on. I simply wanted to crawl up in the bed, pull up the covers, and pretend everything was a bad dream. Unfortunately, I couldn't do that, and it wasn't a bad dream.

Denny came back in a few minutes later. He took one look at my face, walked into the kitchen and came back with a wet dish towel.

"What am I supposed to do with this?" I asked.

"Well, for starters, you can wipe off your face so you don't look like that scary Chuckie doll in the movies. The second thing is I'm trying to get in touch with my guys to see where they relocated the girls to from the hospital."

I cocked an eyebrow at him.

"For safety reasons. But why your info is already on the news is a little baffling since Dimwit knows you're back in town, even though he hasn't come by, and he knows where you live and, more importantly, he's had nothing to do with entire egg thing.

"Parker, this whole thing is beyond strange. What the heck is going on?"

I shook my head and said, "I don't know, Denny, I just don't know."

CHAPTER 24

I called Missy to see if she had any ideas of why I was on the news, again.

"Parker, Parker, Parker. Girl, there are better ways of having fun down there." She sounded a little resigned. "But I do have some good news for you. Gracie Blanche, Flo, and Myrtle Sue are fine."

"Where, where are they?" I hoarsely whispered. My emotions were still on massive overload.

Denny had only seen me cry once in all of the years we've worked together and that was when my precious little Angel dog died. I had also broken out in the worst case of shingles my doctor had ever seen.

I hate emotions. They make me feel things I don't want to feel. I prefer to compartmentalize everything it just makes life so much simpler. Plus, I don't have to deal with anything. I drove my therapist crazy because she wanted me to 'feel things.' I have no clue why I keep seeing her other than I just want to talk to someone who legally and professionally can't stab me in the back. Well, there is that pesky clause in my insurance policy that insists I see someone twice a year.

Yeah, I've got trust issues. So, what?

"Denny's guys moved them to Misty Dawn's house." She took a deep breath. "Their cell phones were jammed and they called me from Misty Dawn's house. That house is like a fortress. No one is going to be able to get to them.

"According to my report, Flo and Myrtle Sue are saying they are ready to rumble but Gracie Blanche is still recovering and is probably going to be doing that for a while."

I smiled. The good news was no one was dead. The bad news was Flo and Myrtle Sue were going to be moving very slowly for a while, but I was glad they were on their way back to us.

If someone had the capability to jam cell phones and create all sorts of havoc from a tech standpoint, then they had the capability to have others do their dirty work for them. Who were these guys?

"Hey, hold on for a second, I'm getting a call from Anatoly."

Really? What incredible timing...and very strange.

"Good morning, Mr. Petrov."

"So, now it's Mister Petrov when before it was Anatoly." He chuckled, "You are a strange woman, Ms. Bell."

"Possibly. What can I do for you?"

"Do you have any knowledge of where my Fabergé Easter Egg is?"

Now it's *his* egg. His ego knows no bounds.

"No clue."

"Ms. Bell, I am prepared to pay a large sum to you...personally, not your company...to any bank in the world if you will tell me where it is."

"Mr. Petrov, as I stated before, I don't have the egg, I haven't even seen this egg so I don't even know if it actually exists, I don't know anything about it. Somehow, I have been pulled into this whole thing and I have absolutely no clue why me, of all people, is in the middle of this."

Changing tactics, I said, "Why do you keep trying to kill and harm my friends? If I knew where the egg was, I would have given you that information several days ago, BUT I don't know anything. All I do know is someone is trying to kill me and my friends over this egg and none of us know anything about it."

A slight pause. "Call me when you know something." And the phone call ended.

Punching the hold button, Missy was still patiently waiting on me.

"Did you find out anything on Anatoly's background?"

"Parker, I'm still trying to fill in the gaps here, but his background does look interesting."

"What does that mean?" I demanded.

"It means he definitely has a tie-in to the royal family, the tsars, but that I don't have enough information yet to give you a definite answer on anything."

"Okay, changing subjects, tell Andrew I'm going to need him to translate Russian into English for me. See what his re-action is and let me know."

"Okay. Parker, I've ordered another pre-fab home for you and it should be put up tomorrow." A slight pause. "Please don't have this one blown up. It costs a lot to get a new one set up quickly."

"I need to move back to Atlanta then. I swear, crazy things happen every single time I'm down here.

"Of course, I do appreciate your not turning my place into a Lady Gatorettes compound...or, did you?" I held my breath.

"No, I did not." She laughed. "I had better sense. It's one thing for them to hang out at your place but it would be chaos if everyone all lived together. I didn't want to encourage that."

"Bless you!" I was delighted I didn't have to share my living space with them. As a computer nerd and book author, I enjoyed my peace and calmness. It never seemed like I had *any* quiet time when I was here. Craziness abounded.

I quickly outlined what Denny and I had planned.

Missy was quiet and then laughed. "I think that might just work, Parker. It's a crazy idea but I think it just might work."

I hoped her comments weren't the kiss of death on the idea.

CHAPTER 25

"Chauncey, Mathilde called." Anne's eyes sparkled as she finished listening to the voicemail. "She says she wants to come visit, but her health precludes her traveling so she wants us to come see her...next weekend. She's offering to pay for our plane fare. What do you think?"

Chauncey stroked his mustache a few times while he was thinking. Finally, he said, "Did she say what she wanted?"

Anne shook her head no.

"Hummm," he mused as he was taking off his backpack. Placing his hat carefully next to the backpack on the couch, he sat down in his chair and continued to stroke his mustache. "Well, we haven't seen her in five years and haven't heard from her in two, so I wonder what she wants and what she's up to.

"For her to offer to pay for us to come see her, well, that's very unusual and strange at best." He continued thinking for a moment. "Okay, you call her back and say I've agreed to it. See what she says after that."

Anne smiled, "Will you talk to her if she asks?"

Chauncey chuckled, "Sure, why not?"

Anne dialed, waited a moment, and with a chipper voice said, "Mathilde? How are you, dear? Yes, yes, I did speak with Chauncey and he said that would be fine. You would like to speak with him? One moment."

Chauncey stroked his mustache a couple of times before taking the phone from Anne's outstretched hand.

"Hello. How are you doing? Yes, we'll be happy to come up and see you. Any particular reason?" A long pause, "Really? Okay, email me the information and we'll see you in eight days. Yes, yes, thanks, you too."

He hung up the phone and said, "I wish I had never had my picture taken with the egg."

Anne slightly smiled. "I'm not going to say 'I told you so' if that makes you feel any better."

"Humph," snorted Chauncey as he picked up the daily crossword puzzle.

CHAPTER 26

I was nervous about meeting these Russian guys. Stupid made for unpleasant surprises and I, for one, did not want to have them suddenly decide that I needed to go on an airplane ride with them.

They landed about ten minutes late which only served to increase my desire to buy more stock in lady's underarm deodorant. Plus, the weather in Florida was alternating between hot and burning-in-Hades hot. Oh, did I mention the humidity level rarely, ever drops below ninety-seven percent? I was always hot, sticky, and sweated enough a small child could swim in the puddles I left behind while walking.

"Ya, you Parker Bell?" shouted a short, fat man with a heavy Russian accent waddling toward me.

I nodded. As he came closer, I stuck out the box for him to have.

He laughed. "No, no, *you* open the box. I don't want to go boom."

I snorted, so ladylike I know. "Seriously, you think I'd blow you up and destroy the egg? Okay, here."

Gently opening the box, I showed him the egg. I closed the lid and handed him the box.

"Now, will you leave me and my friends alone?" I snapped.

Without answering, he turned and waddled back up the airplane steps. I watched as the plane took off. Grinning, I walked back into the airport building.

"Anything going on, guys?" I cheerfully asked.

Denny smiled, nodded, and led me out to the party wagon before speaking.

"Yes, they think they have pulled a fast one on you and are planning on selling the egg to..."

"Anatoly Petrov," I finished the sentence for him.

He nodded yes.

"Well, the good news is we now know for sure that they aren't Anatoly's guys."

He nodded again.

"The question still remains who do these guys work for? As stupid as they seem to be, I don't think they would have come up with this all on their own.

"Also, guys like this don't normally have the financial resources to hire a private plane."

Denny agreed. "Somewhere along the line, Parker, they will mention a name and that's when we can start tracking him...or her...down."

Oh, great! Another possibility of a different player. Here all along I've been thinking it was a man behind the scenes, maybe it was possible a woman was doing this. Why, oh why, did he throw another monkey wrench in the works?

He saw the wheels turning in my head. "You are always arguing for the equality between men and women. It could be a woman just as well as a man orchestrating this."

I hated to admit it but he, cough, cough, might be right.

"What woman would have the most to gain out of all of this? What woman has access to enough money she could do all of this?" I mused.

"Probably any female CEO in the world," snorted Denny.

Rolling my eyes, I said, "I know that. What I meant was who would want an egg like this? There's got to be something we're missing. It's got to be something that is so incre-dibly simple we're overlooking."

Denny laughed, "So, you're going with the Occam's Razor theory?"

I nodded. "Problems are caused by over-complicating things, right? So, the solutions are usually incredibly simple, like that time..."

"Parker, we don't have time for one of your computer security stories. Oh, wait, I'm getting buzzed." He answered his cell phone, nodded a couple of times, and then hung up. "Have you ever heard of someone named Princess Mathilde?"

I shook my head no. "I wonder if Missy has though. Who is this person?"

"Vasily heard them say they were doing this for Princess Mathilde. I don't recall any modern princesses by that name."

Dialing Missy, I wondered about the name Mathilde. It was probably Dutch, I surmised.

"Hello, Parker." She was sounding way too chirpy today. She had probably taken another continuing education course at the Katie Couric school of perkiness. I don't like Katie. "Andrew translated the Russian and, you'll probably find this very interesting, there was a reference to a Princess Mathilde."

"Really?" I was a little surprised.

"Yes, and here's where it gets really interesting. Andrew remembered hearing something about a Princess Mathilde when he was a child. So, he called his mother and asked her if she had ever heard of this princess. Turns out his mother actually knew someone referred to as Princess Mathilde when she worked in the Kremlin. This woman was referred to as a princess, but she wasn't an actual born princess. She wasn't born into the royal lineage."

I was gleeful. Now we were getting somewhere.

"Was she Dutch?" I asked.

"Probably not," answered Missy. "The name is of Germanic origin, although I suppose it's possible. Anyway, that was all the information Andrew could get from his mother. He said she wasn't very forthcoming even with that little bit. Apparently, Russians aren't very open with sharing much of anything even to family members."

"Not surprising considering family members often turn each other in to the KGB to save their own lives," I retorted. "Well, tell him to keep plugging away.

"Wait! He asked his mother, right?" I was excited.

"Yes."

"Perhaps this confirms his mother might have been a courtesan?" I was hopeful.

"Not necessarily, Parker, although that's a thought. I can't imagine a young man would want to know that about his mother."

I groaned. Well, there was *that* factor. I wouldn't want to know that about my mother either. "Perhaps his dad knows something."

"I'll ask."

Hanging up the phone, I gave all of the information to Denny. We were both perplexed.

"Do you think this is all just random coincidence?" I asked.

Denny looked at me. "What do you think?"

"I don't believe in coincidences."

CHAPTER 27

Opulent didn't begin to describe Mathilde's Paris apartment. To say Louis XIV would be impressed and jealous of her décor would be a massive understatement. While the Queen of England might have even given a royal nod to her artistic expression, the influence was all Romanov. Simple, elegant, exquisite leaving no doubt as to her Russian preference for the finer things of life from days gone by.

While she had an entire floor to herself she actually only used two or three rooms on a regular basis. Sipping on her beloved Russian tea, she never could understand why Americans preferred coffee.

She mused that Chauncey was far more likely to want to come to Paris because of the free trip rather than to see her but she knew he'd stop and stay in London for a day before coming to Paris. After all, that was the way she'd arranged his plane tickets.

She was pretty sure Anne and Chauncey would stop and see a couple of old friends regardless of how tired they might be from the plane flight. She had already made arrangements for them to be tailed upon arriving at Heathrow.

While not as nearly flushed with money as she had once been, Mathilde did know how to use her contacts wisely and her money judiciously. She chuckled to herself, "Men are so easy to manipulate, regardless of their age or nationality."

As a former Russian courtesan, she was well-versed in the ways of men. The more powerful they were, the easier they were to manipulate. Money was never an issue for them, loss of ego or embarrassment, on the other hand, was. Less wealthy men thought in terms of money and their sphere of influence was much smaller. Why waste time playing and catching minnows when you could catch a whale? She wasn't interested in catching sharks because after you caught them, they'd have to be killed. It was so unattractive and unladylike to have scores of dead men in your wake. Plus, it made other whales highly suspicious and she never wanted that.

She smiled as she sipped her tea. She had outlived Tsar Nicholas II, Grand Duke Andrei Vladimirovich, Grand Duke Sergei Mikhailovich, and other political figures. She had watched and learned from the best. She was often in the room when one of these powerful men was plotting and planning against his enemies.

Because she was female, young, very attractive, from Poland, and had been appointed as the prima ballerina of the Saint Petersburg Imperial Theatres, none of the men took her presence seriously and she was often overlooked when they were discussing affairs of the state. She might as well as have been a frozen fly on the wall, and, in essence, that is exactly what she was.

As sweet and innocent as she looked, she was ruthless when it came to ousting the artistic director of the Imperial Theatres because he didn't want her as the starring ballerina. She used her influence with her Russian nobility paramours to have him removed as well as other ballerinas she perceived as a threat to her popularity with audiences and to her career.

"Would Madame like more tea?" Her maid had quietly entered the room and was waiting for Mathilde to answer.

"Memories," she murmured. "I made history everywhere I went."

"Yes, madame." She knew better than to ask her again about the tea.

Turning to her, Mathilde asked, "Did you know it was my house, my balcony, that Vladimir Lenin addressed the crowds when he returned from Switzerland in 1917?"

"No, madame, I did not."

"Me. I was the most powerful woman in Russia and yet so few people knew about me." Although quietly said, her words were strong, forceful. She smiled, "That was probably a good thing and it is probably what saved my life on several occasions."

The maid had been with her for many years and had never heard Mathilde mention any of this before.

"Be quiet and listen, you'll never know what you'll find out or learn."

"Yes, madame."

"You may go, no more tea for right now. Wait. Has Vova called?"

"No, madame."

"Hum, perhaps he's still in London. No matter. You may go now."

Her only child, Vladimir, held the royal title of Prince Romanovsky-Krasinsky. Nicknamed Vova, he was now residing in London. Allegedly, he used his fluency in many languages as a translator and was a journalist.

Mathilde had been told he was actually a British Intelligence Officer and everything else was a front. While secretly proud of that, she realized that he was a chameleon just as she was. You adapt to survive and thrive.

"Vova learned well." She acknowledged silently to herself. She frowned slightly as she recalled telling the Grand Duke Andrei Vladimirovich that Vova was his. Never one hundred percent sure of who his real father was as he was growing up, Vladimirovich or since his mother had decades-long affairs with both of them, Vova had a somewhat contentious relationship with her.

When he was a child, she often thought of her son as weak but when he was arrested by the Gestapo in 1941 for refusing to support the Germans in the war with Russia and then spent one hundred forty-four days in a concentration camp she had to re-evaluate her opinion of him. They still maintained a cordial but somewhat distant relationship.

Fluent in a number of languages, Mathilde moved to Paris after the Russian Revolution. While not as wealthy as she once was, she still maintained a lavish apartment and had flourished with her diplomatic connections. She was still a woman who could make things happen.

"Now, Chauncey is a totally different type of man than Vova." She mused. "No matter. I'm sure he doesn't suspect a thing."

CHAPTER 28

"What's the connection, Denny? What are we missing here?" I was totally perplexed. "It's gotta be something simple."

"I know this is going to make you crazy."

I cocked an eyebrow at him. I didn't like the sound of that.

"Why not do a brainstorming session with the Lady Gatorettes..."

"Whoa, ho! Have you lost your ever-loving mind?!" I borderline screeched. "Don't you realize all of the problems I have every time I come to Po Ho...and it's all because of them?"

Denny laughed. "Well, they *did* save your life. That oughta count for something."

I harrumphed and stomped my feet, truly an attractive way for a so-called grownup to act but whatever, but in the end I agreed it might be a good thing to do.

Seriously? What the fongoo was I thinking when I agreed to that?! The jury's still out, and please don't send me any letters with your suggestions either.

CHAPTER 29

I texted Missy Dawn and cordially – choke, choke – invited the Lady Gatorettes over the next day to my new house. Missy had assured me it would be completely set up by ten a.m. at the latest. I invited the gals over for an extended brainstorming lunch at noon to be on the safe side. I knew if there was food involved and if the house still wasn't completed by the time they were ready to eat, the guys setting up my new modular were not going to like the results. Truly, there was a method in my madness.

Missy called. "Parker, your house is almost finished, and I've ordered ten large pizzas to be delivered at noon."

"What kind of pizzas did you order? Because I have absolutely no idea what these gals like and the last thing I want to have happen is a food war because the right pizzas weren't ordered."

I shuddered even thinking of what thrown pizza in my new abode might look like. Red pizza sauce on my ceiling was not something I wanted to experience, and, while pepperoni as a kitchen backsplash sort of held a certain appeal, I wasn't into redneck kitsch. I simply didn't trust those five hormonal women when it came to food and what they wanted.

Missy laughed. "Parker, no worries. I found out what each of them liked to eat on their pizza, ordered it, they'll have their name on the box, and everything should be fine. Once I explained it was for the Lady Gatorettes, the pizza place was, shall we say, more than accommodating to make sure the right pizza goes to the right person. Those girls do have their reputation."

How well I knew that! AND, I wanted to stay on their good side.

"You're awesome, Missy!" Oops, that slipped out. I rarely complimented Missy and it embarrassed both of us when that unfortunate occurrence happened. Typically, we both ignored my faux pas.

Per our standard protocol, she ignored me and continued, "I ordered enough pizza for you, Denny, and the Lady Gatorettes. Depending on whether John Boy shows up or not, you'll have two or three extra pizzas."

She coughed softly. "I'm guessing a couple of those gals might eat more than one whole large pizza."

Yeah, well, there's that. Those gals do have hefty appetites.

"Do you know anything more on Princess Mathilde?" I asked.

"Actually, I think I do." She paused, and I could hear her typing on her keyboard. "Here it is. Her real name is Princess Mathilde Romanovskaya-Krasinskaya and she became a princess after her marriage to Grand Duke Andrei Vladimirovich who, by the way, was a cousin to Tsar Nicholas the second."

"Whoa!" I was surprised.

Ignoring my interruption, Missy continued, "Apparently, she had a thing for royalty because she was a courtesan to Nicholas, the Grand Duke Sergei Mikhailovich and the Grand Duke Andrei Vladimirovich, both of whom were cousins of Nicholas. She was also the head prima ballerina and used her influence to work her way up into the royalty hemisphere.

"Oh, yeah, she was from Poland. Her father and brother were very well-known dancers there and that's how she ended up dancing in Russia and gaining the attention of Russian nobility."

Unbelievable. I simply shook my head.

"So, is it possible she has or had a Fabergé Egg?" I asked. I didn't realize I was holding my breath as I waited on her answer.

"Well," Missy said slowly. "I suppose it's possible but there's virtually no way of telling that."

"Okay, thanks." I hung up. This had just gotten a lot more interesting...and a lot more confusing. Maybe it was a good thing the Lady Gatorettes were coming over.

Involuntarily, I shuddered. What was happening in Po'thole where everything was crazy anyway and it only appeared to be getting worse. I think I feel a headache coming on.

CHAPTER 30

After clearing customs at Heathrow International Airport, Anne and Chauncey put their backpacks on and made their way to the exiting gate area.

Stroking his mustache, Chauncey slowly turned his head surveying the madding rush of passengers in one of the busiest airports in the world.

"Two o'clock, man holding up the sign that says Flowers family," said Chauncey quietly not looking directly at Anne.

"Female, dark hair, dark jacket at nine o'clock," said Anne pretending to look at her boarding pass and then glancing around at the flight boards prominently displayed everywhere.

"Ready?"

"Yes."

Looking like the typical confused or lost mature passengers, they walked over to the guy holding the sign. He was ignoring them.

"Excuse me, do you know how to get to the luggage area? We're from the States and we're not sure where to go." Chauncey was smiling.

Anne had turned around looking at the throng of people, turned back to Chauncey and appeared to lose her balance. She bumped him and he stumbled into the sign guy.

"Hey, watch it!" snapped the man. "It's downstairs, just follow the crowd."

"Anne, be careful! My apologies," smiled Chauncey, "and thank you."

The man just nodded and held his sign up again.

"My turn," said Anne gleefully.

They walked over to the girl who appeared to be playing a game on her phone. Anne walked up very close to her.

"Excuse me, dear, but my husband really needs to use the restroom...the loo, I believe you call it...and I don't see any signs anywhere. Where would it be?"

Chauncey interrupted her. "Anne, is that Billy over there?"

All three of them turned to look at some unsuspecting tourist.

"Nope, never mind, I thought that was him but it's not." Leaning over to them, he whispered, "Where is the bathroom?"

The girl pointed about thirty feet away. "There."

"Thank you."

Anne and Chauncey went into the proper restrooms, came out and promptly sat down in the chairs at the gate closest to the restroom. Without looking at each other, they both pulled out a book and proceeded to read it.

Where they were sitting they could keep an eye on both the girl and the guy.

Anne started to laugh, pointing at something in her book, she leaned over to Chauncey to show him, whispering, "I think they're confused and don't know what to do. They can't stay in those spots forever."

Chauncey laughed heartily and pointed his finger at Anne's book. "I think we need to stay at least thirty minutes, then go to the luggage area, and leave from there."

"Sounds good to me."

They both went back to reading their books but keeping a discreet but diligent eye on the man and the woman. After fifteen minutes, they observed them becoming agitated, unsure of what to do and they kept looking at their watches. Then the man walked over to the woman and they talked for a moment. He shrugged, she shrugged, they looked at Anne and Chauncey who appeared to be deeply engrossed in their books, they talked for a few minutes and then left.

Anne and Chauncey never looked up for another fifteen minutes. Then Chauncey said, "Shall we?"

Anne smiled, put her book back into her backpack, and said, "Of course. Luggage area?"

He nodded.

They took their time in exiting the airport terminal, bypassing the luggage area since they had only brought their backpacks with them. The weather was typical English weather – cold, windy, with a lot of bone-chilling dampness in the air. They looked around and Anne raised her hand for a cab.

The London taxi slid to a stop in front of them. "Any luggage?" asked the driver through the open window.

They shook their head 'no' as they climbed in the spacious cab. Chauncey gave the driver an address. The cabbie turned around, looked at them for a moment, and then started driving.

"Let me know if you think anyone is following us," said Chauncey quietly. The cabbie nodded, his eyes flickering to the rearview mirror to observe Anne and Chauncey, and then to watch the road.

A few minutes later, he said, "Mate, I believe we're being followed but they're ahead of us. See that brown car? Two cars up on the right side? When I change lanes, they change lanes. When I slow down, they slow down.

"Hope you don't mind my saying so, but if you're being followed by cars being in the front rather than behind, then you're being tracked by some pretty sophisticated people."

"What's your background?" asked Anne, leaning forward in her seat and smiling.

He grinned back. "If I told you, I'd have to kill you."

Anne laughed and clapped her hands. "Mission Impossible, is that it?"

He laughed.

Becoming serious, Anne asked, "So have you been assigned to us?"

He smiled.

"What's your name?" she asked.

He glanced back at them. "Robert. And, no, I don't go by Bob or Rob."

"Robert, do you think you can lose the car without being too obvious about it?" asked Chauncey.

Robert pulled the cab over, put it in reverse, and backed into an unseen driveway. He continued to back rapidly down the driveway and then backed into an alleyway. He turned the car off.

"Probably." Leaning over the car seat, he winked. "How do you want to play this, Mr. Livingstone?"

CHAPTER 31

The good news was my house was finished, the food had arrived...hot, and the Lady Gatorettes were chowing down on their very own special pizzas. It was a good day in the neighborhood. Of course, we hadn't started the brainstorming session and, goodness knows, how that was going to play out.

Pizza boxes were scattered around the dining table and everyone had staked out a spot in the living room to eat their pizza. I had a slice of pepperoni halfway to my mouth when the inevitable happened.

Myrtle Sue was on one side of the table and Mary Jane was on the other. In between them was an unopened box of pizza. Unfortunately, they were trying to jerk it away from the other one.

While Myrtle Sue was normally far more restrained than the other members of the Lady Gatorettes when it came to confrontations and showdowns, apparently pizza brought out her more aggressive tendencies even though she was moving slowly from her injuries.

"It's mine, Mary Jane!" She growled. "You take your hands off of it right now if you ever expect to use your hands to cook with ever again!"

"Listen, you miserable little Martha Stewart wannabe, it's mine!" snarled Mary Jane.

"Um, guys, there's two pizzas left. Why don't y'all split them?" I obviously did not know the pizza rules of etiquette.

Looking like something from the exorcist, they both whipped their heads around to glare at me for a moment and then went back into their demonic stare-down contest. At this moment, I was hungry and, more importantly, I had better sense than to continue to talk to them when it involved food.

Rhonda Jean heaved herself up out of her chair and went over to the table. She smiled at both of them and then snatched it from them. She opened the lid quickly and licked the top of the pizza. They screamed and were using language the Navy SEALs would have been proud of.

While it was entertaining, I was still hungry, and I still continued to put pizza in my mouth. I harbored no illusions that they could snatch up my pizza and eat it as a consolation prize. I wanted to be sure it was finished before that thought occurred to them.

Misty Dawn glanced over at me and said, "You look like you're eating at a food trough. Slow down, they're not going to eat your pizza."

Grrr! I hate it when it appears she's reading my mind. However, I did slow down so I could enjoy my pizza.

"Smart move, Rhonda Jean! However, I saw what you actually did," grinned Misty Dawn. "Myrtle Sue, you get three slices from that box. Mary Jane, you get three slices from the other box. The rest of us," looking at Rhonda Jean and Flo, "will split the rest."

"Euwww, no!" squealed Myrtle Sue. "Rhonda Jean done licked the top of it! I don't want her dog germs!"

Rhonda Jean put down the pizza and sent killing eye darts at her. "Are you calling me a not nice word, Myrtle Sue? If so, I hope you enjoyed that last bite of pizza you had 'cas it will be the last of anything you eat!"

Mary Jane popped up with, "I'll eat it. I like Rhonda Jean." And grinned.

Misty Dawn snapped, "Myrtle Sue, you better not be calling Rhonda Jean...or anyone of us bad names. Plus, Rhonda Jean did not lick the top of the pizza, she only made it look that way."

She looked around at each of the girls in turn, nodded, and said, "Because you know what that means."

Glad they did, I wasn't sure but hoped it didn't mean someone's unfortunate permanent demise.

Everyone nodded, although, Myrtle Sue and Mary Jane were still giving each other the redneck evil stink eye. I was glad I wasn't in their direct line of fire eye gaze. That look they were giving each other could be used as rocket fuel to send someone to the moon and back.

"Rhonda Jean, put three slices on each plate and then split up the rest with us."

I cleared my throat, "Now that we have that out of the way..."

"You ain't the boss of us," growled Flo.

Much as I'd like to attribute her grouchiness to her getting out of the hospital and being full of pain meds, I surmised it had more to do with her thinking I was taking over Misty Dawn's leadership role. Nothing could be further from the truth.

Oh, mercy, what did I inadvertently just do?! My fuse, which is never long anyway, snapped.

"Awright, listen up! You're in *my* home, eating *my* food, and as invited guests I expect a certain amount of pleasantness in *my* home. While I am NOT your boss, you are in *my* home. Stop acting like big overgrown babies! Eat the pizza and listen up."

Dead silence. They were all looking at me...with shark eyes and then laughter.

"Yep, yep." "For sure." "Okay." "This had better be good." "Yes."

Denny was still sitting back away from the girls and threw me a thumbs up. Okay, I must be doing okay, although I vaguely wondered if they turned on me, would Denny jump to my rescue. Probably but I wasn't willing to bet money on it. I'd have to ask him later.

"Okay, here's what I know at this point in time. More importantly, wait until I finish before giving me your opinion or suggestion on anything. Got it?" I looked around and they nodded.

"I suddenly start getting calls about this mysterious Fabergé Easter Egg. I know little to nothing about these eggs. All I know is they were made for the Russian Tsar Nicholas II way back when.

"By the way, where is Gracie Blanche?"

"She's in rehab," said Flo. Raising her hand because she could see I was getting ready to ask where. "We, us girls, have our own version of rehab that's quicker and cheaper than Po'thole Healthcare."

I could only imagine.

Denny interjected, "She's not there. She's at an undisclosed location with nurses, physical therapists, occupational therapists, and her own private doctor with around the clock care. She's safe."

I laughed. "Gosh, it sounds like she's at the National Guard Armory."

Denny didn't say anything. I laughed silently to myself. I couldn't believe I had guessed it right off the bat. Either Denny's slipping or I'm getting way better at guessing things. I have to admit, that's a great place for her to be.

"Continuing, Anne and Chauncey seem to have some type of knowledge about this egg, but I don't know the connection. I keep getting calls from Anatoly Petrov, the Russian billionaire businessman about this egg. I had Missy do some research and those guys on the plane have some connection with Mathilde somebody or other who's now living in Paris. She apparently was a courtesan to Tsar Nicholas and his merry band of cousins. She married one of them and produced a son who lives in London.

"My friends were beaten up and ended up in the hospital and the river. What the fongoo is going on here? We need to figure out what's happening. And, contrary to what you guys think of me, I don't want to see any of y'all killed or hurt anymore! My nerves won't take it."

Denny drawled out, "And I didn't think you liked anyone but yourself and yet you used the word 'friends'. My, my!"

The Lady Gatorettes all laughed and did high fives. I was pleased to note that no pepperoni or tomato sauce splattered on my ceiling or walls. They must eat pizza a little bit more daintily than I thought. Will wonders never cease!

"What caused Gracie Blanche to even do research on the Fabergé egg?" asked Misty Dawn. "Or did something just pop in her mind to look up Chauncey on Facebook?"

I stood for a moment, thinking. "You know, I really don't know. Denny…"

"On it." He made a phone call. "She's sleeping. She'll be asked when she wakes up."

"Was Chauncey standing next to the egg or was it actually his? Where was it? I can figure out who to contact on that if I know where." Rhonda Jean stated.

"Where did those Russian bozos rent the plane? If they used a credit card, that can be tracked." Flo winked.

"Give me that Russian slut's full name and I can find out stuff about her that will make her boots shake," grinned Myrtle Sue.

"I have a, um, pen pal in London. What's her son's name again?" asked Mary Jane.

All of the girls turned to look at Mary Jane with their eyebrows raised.

"Really, I do."

"Humph," snorted Flo. "Is this another of your internet boyfriends?"

Mary Jane grinned. "Just get this guy's name and I can get the skinny on him."

"Okay, ladies, let's get it on," said Misty Dawn, clapping her hands. "There is no one, repeat, no one who can out strategize us. It's the fourth quarter, FSU is leading by fourteen. Are we going to let the Gators lose?"

Screams of 'No' permeated the air.

I was amazed. It was like I had my own little version of the CIA. And did I think to put my company computer team on this? But, nooo, I did not. Actually, I try to keep my personal life separate from my business life and, realistically, I did not want any more people knowing about this than Missy and Andrew.

People have a way of gossiping, and things have a way of getting out. Even though my people were well vetted and paid very well to keep secrets, we all know things have a way of escaping. I certainly didn't want anyone in the news world to get hold of what was going on, and especially what was happening in Po'thole.

"Let's do this!" I shouted. "I'm calling Missy so y'all can talk to her."

Just as I was about to call Missy and put her on speaker phone, my phone rang. I groaned when I recognized the number. Why, why, why did she have to call me at the most inopportune times?! Why?!

"Hello, Saffron." My voice was flat. I did not want to encourage her for a long conversation.

"Hellooo, Parker."

Shoot! She sounded way too perky. This never boded well for me.

"Parker, dear, what are you doing down in that little town? Do you have anything for a new book?"

"No, Saffron, I do not."

"Honey, I'll bet you do. Why? Because you haven't called me with any updates on that fancy Fabergé egg and when you don't call me that means you're working on something." Saffron sounded smug. I hate her...well, not really because she always gets me such great deals on books, but she does annoy me greatly.

"Saffron, why? What have you heard?" Then it dawned on me. "Did Gracie Blanche call you again?"

"No, I haven't heard from her either, and she's always so good about returning my phone calls. Not like someone else I could mention. But I did hear you were on the local news down there." She laughed.

I could see her grinning through the phone. I must have had smoke coming out my ears and my eyes crossed because Denny took the phone out of my hand and walked across the room murmuring something to Saffron.

The Lady Gatorettes were busy chattering amongst themselves and I was starting to calm down after taking a couple of big gulps of Coke.

Denny handed me my phone. "I told her I'd have you call her with a fresh, new, exciting book idea in about a week."

He winked, "That just bought you a couple of weeks of peace from her."

"Still doesn't answer who called in that information to the news station," I retorted.

"Relax, apparently it was retracted as fake news that somehow made it on air," said Denny grinning. "It won't happen again."

I just shook my head and called Missy. Warning her, I put her on speaker phone and let loose the girls with their questions. I sat back and finished my pizza.

CHAPTER 32

"So, I'm thinking Anatoly's related to either Mathilde or someone from that time frame," said Myrtle Sue.

"I agree that he's related to someone closely connected to Nicholas," I said. "I do think there's something about this particular Fabergé egg that is personal to him but I'm pretty sure he's not related to Mathilde."

"Remember, this guy came out of nowhere in Russia..."

"No one comes out of nowhere in Russia," snorted Myrtle Sue. "They ALL have pasts, even with all of those crazy names. They can be tracked down."

Much as I hated to admit it, it did make perfect sense and I knew she was right.

"Parker, did you ask Missy to send us the latest laptops?" grinned Denny.

I groaned. "Missy, did you hear that?"

"I'm sending Andrew on Delta, flying first class I might add, into Jacksonville International and he should be arriving just about the time someone's there to pick him up. He's bringing seven fully programmed laptops."

"Ah, there's only five..."

"Parker," she sighed, "I'm guessing you will probably need a new one and I know Denny needs a new one. Five of them and two of you make seven.

"And, Parker, I had Chris set up everything on all the computers."

"Great! What kind of bonus did you give Chris?"

Missy laughed, "What else? A month's supply of gift certificates to Mr. Ho's Chinese restaurant."

"Good going. Thanks. Later."

"Denny, go pick up Andrew at JAX."

"No."

I spun around and looked him dead in the eye. "Why not, mister?"

"Because I need to be here." His eyes flashed. "Send Mary Jane. She'll wheedle more information out of him than any of us ever could."

Well, she did have a surprising way with men. Reluctantly, I asked her to go. To say she was happy was an understatement. I guess talking to a live man in a car for an hour or so was better than skyping with someone overseas.

"We're probably going to be here for hours, probably overnight and all day tomorrow, right?" asked Myrtle Sue.

I nodded.

"I need to go home and fix JW enough food for the next twenty-four hours."

The other gals nodded their agreement and various 'me too's' were heard. Me? Since I don't have anyone special in my life at the moment, these domestic issues never occurred to me.

"Don't worry, Parker, I'll bring enough food back for you and Denny later."

"Yeah, I'll bring a couple of covered dishes," volunteered Flo.

"Yeah, I'll bring something too," said Misty Dawn. Grinning at me, "What? You think I don't know how to cook?"

I found myself feeling gratitude. Quickly I shook it off. It simply wouldn't do for these crazy women to know I was actually touched by their thoughtfulness.

Denny laughed, "Parker's speechless because she didn't think that far in advance on the food thing."

I grumbled, "You could have talked all day without ever saying that, Denny."

"True, but it's so much fun to watch you turn red in the face."

Once all of the Lady Gatorettes had disappeared into their domestic bliss, it was just me and Denny. The quiet and calmness was almost unnerving.

"You know this is only going to last for about three hours, don't you?" asked Denny. He was stretched out on the couch, hands behind his head, and looked relaxed.

I laughed. "Do you honestly think we're going to have three hours of doing nothing? You know how it is here. Every time I come here it's total mayhem and chaos."

"Yeah, but you love it."

Sort of, maybe. It was certainly way more exciting than going from my peaceful condo to my peaceful office in Atlanta. Plus, I was getting bored in Atlanta. Yeah, how could that ever happen, right?

Truth be known, and certainly something I didn't want to admit out loud right now to anyone, but this nutty little town was starting to grow on me. There was always something going on. Yes, it was usually crazy and, yes, I was usually in the middle of it but there was something to be said about bonding with folks I'd known forever and three days...wait, wait, wait! I shook my head. I didn't need to expose those feelings. Feelings I barely knew the words for, much less wanting to experience.

Cautiously I answered him. "Yeah, maybe."

"You know you could actually run your company from here. Missy actually takes care of almost everything up there anyway, even when you're in Atlanta. You've got Chris as the figurehead and everyone thinks he's the managing director when you're not in."

Denny coughed. "Your company isn't set up like most normal companies. You know that, don't you?"

"Yes, I do know that, thank you very much. I deliberately structured it that way. I don't and didn't want my company to be like any other ones. It's at the right size for what I want. I don't want to grow it any bigger. I'm very happy with being a boutique computer security company."

"Would you ever want to sell it?"

I cocked an eyebrow at him. "You making an offer or have someone who wants to make an offer?"

He grinned. "Not me. I don't have the millions it would take to buy it from you. Plus, you think I want to leave all of this fun?" He winked.

A thought flashed through my mind. "Did Petrov contact you about buying my company?"

"Nope. No one has. I was just thinking if you had unlimited cash, you could move down here and never be bothered with city people ever again."

I snorted. "I pretty much have unlimited cash and resources right now. Everything seems to be running smoothly. I don't have any real need or desire to sell it. Plus, and don't take this the wrong way, but you, Missy, and I are all pretty much joined at the hip. I need the cash flow to be able to keep you guys on payroll."

"Really? You don't think I have my own sources of income?" He shook his head. "Parker, Parker, Parker. You're not the only person who knows how to make money or invest wisely."

My short fuse was starting to unravel when a thought entered my mind. I went to the dining room table, scribbled something down on a piece of paper and handed it to him.

"I know talking about money turns you on but, seriously, Parker, I'm never going to sleep with you. Stop unfastening your shirt." He chuckled but pointed a finger at the remote, tapped his watch, and held up two fingers.

Great, my house was bugged, again, and Denny's magical, mystery watch had detected when the device was activated. Apparently about two minutes ago.

I nodded. I pointed at the kitchen and he shook his head 'no.'

"So, you don't want to sell your company?"

"Nope." Changing subjects, I asked, "Does Potus need to go out?"

Potus, who had been lying by the couch, got up, stretched, headed to the back door, and turned around looking at me.

I looked at Denny. His eyes were shut and I rolled mine.

"I saw that."

"No, you did not!"

"Yes, I did but take Potus out anyway."

Opening the door cautiously and sticking my head out carefully – although if someone were going to shoot me, it would be an easy hit – I let Potus out and I followed him at a discreet distance. Hey, I didn't want to embarrass him while he was doing his duty.

"Glad you understood what I meant."

I almost jumped out of my skin.

"How the heck do you do that?" I snapped.

"I'll train you sometime. The good news is that remote was not turned on the entire time everyone was in there. What that means to me is that silence activates it and then it will transmit sound back to wherever. Because your house was never silent for more than fifteen seconds, it didn't have a chance to activate itself."

"But, we were in there, Denny, and we were talking."

"True, but it only activated after we hadn't talked for almost a minute. It's not a sophisticated model."

"We need to get rid of it or de-activate it before everyone gets back."

"Let me have a little fun, would ya?" He grinned. "And keep Potus out here until you hear my signal."

"Sure, go for it." I laughed.

A few minutes later I heard an air horn go off inside my house. This wasn't just any short blast. Oh, no, this was the ear-piercing, head-splitting, never-get-over-it blast. Denny was not only killing whoever was listening in but had also probably destroyed the bug and maybe my remote in the process.

Once the noise had stopped, Potus and I went back into the house to wait on our merry bunch of crazy women and the new laptops.

CHAPTER 33

"Is the weather nice in Paris this time of year?" asked Chauncey, his blue eyes twinkling.

"It's Paris. It's, well, Paris."

Anne and Chauncey smiled at Robert. "So nice to make your acquaintance."

Robert smiled. "Likewise."

"Robert, is Vova expecting us?"

"Yes. There is a board of directors meeting at the Victoria and Albert in about an hour. You'll meet him there. We'll have lunch set up for you and when you're through, I'll take you to the bed and breakfast."

He turned and looked at them. "I'm sure you're tired but this should be concluded within two hours."

"Anything new I need to know about Anatoly Petrov?"

Robert half-laughed, "Well, you're probably not on his Christmas card list but he doesn't dare do anything to you in the States or here since you're officially retired and have been for years. In France, though, that might be a different story."

He cleared his throat. "Might I ask just one question of you, Mr. Livingstone?"

"Chauncey."

"Chauncey, then."

"Yes."

"What made you let a picture be made of you and the Fabergé egg and then have it posted on social media?"

Anne shook her head. "I asked him the same thing."

Chauncey played with his mustache for a few moments, looked at Anne, and then at Robert.

"I really didn't think anyone would notice it and I certainly didn't think it would turn into this debacle."

"You winter in that little town and you weren't aware that you have an antique show-crazed person who follows you on social media?" Robert sounded astonished. "Chauncey, old boy, you must be slipping a little."

A half-smile formed on Chauncey's lips. "Perhaps so."

Robert turned back around in the car. "It's time to go to the V and A."

Pulling around to the back and parking in an employee's parking spot, all three entered the museum through the back unnoticed.

As promised, a nice luncheon had been prepared for them in an office behind where the board meeting was scheduled.

Vova walked into the meeting, said his hellos, and then exited through another door. His presence wasn't missed and, if asked, board members could honestly say he had been there.

Waving his hand at the Livingstones to stay seated, Vova sat down across from them and dug into his meal.

"I trust Robert took very good care of you?" He asked, wiping his mouth gently with the linen napkin.

They nodded.

"I gather you were followed but Robert lost them." It was a statement, not a question.

They nodded again.

"What's the latest?" Vova continued to eat as Chauncey gave his report.

"They were two at the airport, a man and a woman. We planted bugs on both of them. I'm sure if you plug in our old codes, you could probably track them."

Vova slightly smiled and nodded. Chauncey finished with all of the other details.

"Any questions?" he asked.

Leaning back in his chair, his hands delicately wiping his mouth again, Vova said, "So these women, these Lady Gatorettes and Parker Bell, might actually be able to do what the CIA and MI6 have not been able to do?"

Anne smiled, and Chauncey said, "It's totally possible. They're always on a sugar and caffeine high and they live in a small town, but they're not stupid. They're not very sophisticated," he quietly chuckled, "but you don't have to be in our world.

"If Misty Dawn, the leader, gets hold of Anatoly after he tried to have her killed or even if it was Mathilde's guys, they're going to wish they had been sent to Siberia instead of what she and those other gals will do to them."

Vova permitted a slight smile. "They're that good, Chauncey? I don't believe I've ever heard you describe someone like that."

Anne piped up. "They are that good. Had this been years earlier, they could have worked for us."

Vova nodded. "Let's see how this plays out then. Let's continue our original plan."

Standing up, he said, "I need to get back to the meeting. You still have the number if anything goes awry?"

Chauncey and Anne both nodded and tapped their heads.

"Cheers then."

CHAPTER 34

M ary Jane tapped on the front door and opened it before I could even shout 'hello.' She carried in three laptops and a very disheveled Andrew carrying the other four laptops.

Mary Jane smiled broadly. "Got it."

After looking at Andrew, I almost felt sorry for him. An hour and a half of non-stop questions and jabbering from Mary Jane in an enclosed car would cause almost anyone, including Denny, to beg for mercy. Andrew never had a chance.

The poor guy looked like he had been ridden hard and hung up wet. He wearily followed Mary Jane over to the dining room table and plopped the computers down. He cleared his throat, looking around, "May I have something to drink? Anything will do."

"Beer, Coke, or iced tea?" asked Denny.

He was wearing his poker face. Oh, great, we're going to be playing good cop, bad cop. I decided to play along. If Andrew knew anything about anything, he'd soon be giving it up.

I smiled. "Andrew, so glad you volunteered to bring the laptops. It will be a nice break from the office."

He looked panic-stricken. "I don't know anything, Parker. I swear I don't. I gave all of the information I had to Missy. Mary Jane seems to think I'm working with Anatoly Petrov. I swear I don't know anything."

He looked about ready to cry. I inwardly sighed. This guy was already broken and I seriously doubted we were going to get much information from him; however, it might be worth a try.

"Out!" I shouted at Mary Jane and Denny, catching them both off-guard. "Everybody out!"

"Hey!" They both protested.

"Out, until I say you can come back in...and that goes for everyone else! NO ONE comes back in *my* house until I say so!" I hoped I looked appropriately mean and irritated. Okay, mad would work here too.

"Take Potus with you."

"Parker," Denny drawled, "you might want to let the dog stay."

"No, he goes too. He's got big ears." I wanted to let Denny know that I knew about Potus' special collar with the hidden microphone.

Denny slammed the door on his way out. So, he's a big baby. What else is new?

Turning back to Andrew who was seated at the table now and starring at the laptops, I said, "Bottled water okay?"

He nodded his head. I went into the kitchen, got us two bottled waters, and gave him one.

"Tell me what you know," I gently prodded.

"Please don't make me ride back with Mary Jane. I'll have to kill myself." He said quietly, desperately.

I smiled. "You won't have to. I'll get Denny or someone else to take you back to the airport tomorrow.

"Now, tell me about you and what you know."

He nodded, took a big gulp of water, and started talking. "My dad was an economist and applied to teach at Berkeley. He was accepted and he brought my mother and me over. She had worked as an attaché at the Russian consulate. Once here, she didn't like California, had Russian friends here in Atlanta, and decided to move."

He looked up at me. "My parents didn't get along but decided it was best to have a marriage of sorts and they would split custody with me.

"Of course, since they had been at the highest levels of Russian government and saw and heard things, they were automatically suspected of being spies in this country. They weren't, aren't. They just wanted a better life for themselves and for me."

Taking another sip of water, he continued, "I honestly don't think they know very much about the Fabergé egg. My mother knew of Mathilde and probably actually met her once or twice but, other than that, I don't think she had any interaction with her.

"My dad obviously knows of Anatoly Petrov and the rumors that he's trying to manipulate the international money markets but, other than that, I don't believe he's ever met the man."

Whoa! My ears picked up on the 'manipulate the international money markets' because this was the first I'd heard of it but, then again, that wasn't what I'd been focusing on.

Changing tactics, I asked, "What do you do after work, Andrew?"

Holding up my hand and smiling, "I know, technically and legally, I can't ask you that, but I would like for you to volunteer that information."

He looked surprised. "I thought you knew. I thought everybody knew. I volunteer at the Salvation Army three nights a week, two nights a week I volunteer at the emergency animal hospital, and the other two nights I either go to the movies or stay home and read."

He laughed self-consciously, looked down and then back up at me. "I'm actually kind of boring. I like helping homeless people, they have some great stories. Most of them are just really down on their luck and just want someone to listen to them and make them feel like they matter to someone. And I love animals."

I blinked. Wow. I had a real-life humanitarian working for me. Goes to show never judge a book by its cover. I was fully aware he could be a spy in sheep's clothing but somehow I didn't think so. I believe Andrew's on the up and up.

"Did you bring a change of clothes to fly back in the morning or something else?"

"Yes, I have a small backpack in the car. Missy told me I was spending the night at the Holiday Inn Express and that someone would pick me up around ten a.m. to take me back to the airport. Once I got back in Atlanta, I could have the rest of the day off."

I was beyond delighted that Missy had the foresight to get him a hotel room and also have him totally out of our hair.

I said, "I'll have one of Denny's guys pick you up at ten, that way you can sleep in a little bit."

I was reasonably sure Denny probably already had his room bugged just on the off chance he was bogus. I didn't think so but, then again, I've been wrong before...not that I would ever willingly admit it.

Opening the door, I discovered all of the Lady Gatorettes were sitting on the deck eating doughnuts. They were licking their fingers when they saw me. All of them licked their fingers quickly and stuck their hands out like small children who were getting ready to have their mother wipe their hands.

Denny grinned and winked at me. "Spraying now, ladies." He sprayed something on their hands and as they twisted their hands in a washing motion, he tossed little towelettes to them.

"Okay, their hands are clean now for their new laptops."

Jumping to their feet and squealing with delight, they all bum rushed me and Denny and scooted through the door. I could see Andrew backing into the kitchen away from this mayhem.

More squeals of delight as they found the box with their name on it. Opening up the boxes, you would have thought they had won the Florida Lottery.

"Oh, look! Mine's purple, my favorite color!"

"Mine's red!"

"Mine's seafoam green!"

"Blue!"

"Gun metal grey!"

Silently laughing to myself, I knew Missy had found out their favorite colors and had the laptops covers changed to reflect their own individual tastes. Also, that was one way to keep them from fighting over which laptop belonged to whom.

Denny walked over to Andrew. "Ready to go?"

Still looking somewhat shell-shocked, Andrew just nodded.

"Bye, Andrew!" shouted Mary Jane. "Thanks for everything!" And she, oh just gag me with a spoon, blew him a kiss. The other Lady Gatorettes all made smoochy smoochy kissing sounds. Andrew barreled out the front door. Denny grinned, turned at the door, and made a slight bow to the girls.

They hooted and catcalled at him.

"Ladies, ladies!" I said, clapping my hands, "We've had some fun. Now it's time to get down to brass tacks. Let's figure out what's going on here."

I don't think a beehive had any more activity going on than what these gals were doing. Cell phone calls were being made, skype sessions were going on, and obscure information was being googled.

"Got something." Rhonda Jean pushed back from the dining room table. Misty Dawn was at the other end of the table and looked over at Rhonda Jean. Mary Jane and Flo were in the living room and looked up. Myrtle Sue was hunkered over her computer on the kitchen countertop, nodded, and then glanced up.

"Whatcha got?" I asked, hoping that something somewhere had fallen through the cracks and we could finally figure out what was going on and what the connections were.

Rhonda Jean smiled. "I'm feeling faint. I don't know if I can tell you anything without...a snack."

Everyone groaned. I, on the other hand, thought I had seen some frozen doughnuts in my freezer. Unless the girls had found and devoured them, they were still in my freezer.

"Hold up. Let me look at something." I went over and opened the freezer door and lo and behold there were actually a dozen doughnuts in there just waiting to be microwaved. I held the box up.

"Tell us and I'll put the doughnuts in the microwave. You can have first pick."
I grinned wickedly.

Rhonda Jean had a big smile on her face. "Okay, here's what I found out. Anne and Chauncey went to an antique show in Bangor, Maine. A friend of theirs had a booth and Chauncey offered to loan her the Fabergé egg for display only, hoping that it would increase his friend's antique sales.

"The friend took the picture of Chauncey standing next to the egg and posted it on Facebook. She tagged Chauncey, which is how Gracie Blanche discovered it, probably by accident. You know how things come and go on Facebook. It doesn't appear that she was actually stalking him."

Humm, I might have to apologize to Gracie Blanche after accusing her of stalking. I'll think about it.

"Chauncey's friend thought the egg was a good replica but since she only specializes in silver and china this wasn't her area of expertise."

"You didn't tell her otherwise, did you?" asked Misty Dawn.

Rhonda Jean shook her head no. "I asked if she thought it was real and she said, 'Probably not. Anne and Chauncey have traveled the world and they probably picked it up in some souvenir place.' I agreed with her."

"Everyone else report in on what you've got," ordered Misty Dawn. "Then I think we can all grab a couple of hours sleep."

Inwardly, I groaned. A houseful of sleeping Lady Gatorettes was not something I really wanted to wake up to; however, I knew if anyone tried to break in, the intruder would die in a heartbeat.

"Good work, Rhonda Jean. Flo, whatcha got?"

"Parker, I finally found out those guys rented the airplane down at Daytona. They didn't use a credit card though, they paid cash."

"Cash? And the rental place let them take off in it?" I was confused.

Flo laughed. "They were not quite that trusting, Parker. They took a credit card and then when the guys came back that's when they paid in cash."

I lifted my eyebrows.

"It was a pre-paid, reloadable American Express Bluebird card," laughed Flo. "Apparently the plane guys didn't know that. They saw American Express on the card and made the very dangerous assumption that AmX would pay in case the plane was absconded. They wouldn't but those bozos didn't know that."

She held up hand, "Before you ask, the name on the card is...M. Mouse."

That set all of the girls off in peals of laughter.

"Mickey Mouse!"

"M-i-c...see you soon!"

"K-e-y!"

"M-o-u-s-e!"

"Mickey Mouse! Mickey Mouse!"

Even I had to grin at that. Denny cracked up as well. He had been quietly texting messages after he returned from dropping off Andrew as the girls worked.

Wiping away the tears of laughter from my eyes, I asked, "Mary Jane?"

"Still trying to get ahold of my guys."

"Myrtle Sue?"

"Mathilde has a very fascinating background and it's taking a little bit of time to read between the lines and track down her connection."

Misty Dawn yawned and said, "The research on Anatoly is interesting. He appears out of nowhere and then disappears. Parents appear and then disappear. He may have worked for the old KGB at some point, but it also looks like he's been in and out of the country, ours, a number of times. I'm trying to track down dates."

"What about you, Parker? What have you found out?" asked Flo.

"There's a lot more to this particular egg than what appears on the surface. It would appear that it went from Russia to Turkey to England and then came to the U.S., to Vermont.

"This particular egg may be one of the missing ones from the Fabergé collection and would be, therefore, quite valuable from a historical standpoint, if nothing else."

"Let's take a four-hour sleep break and then get back at it again," said Misty Dawn. "It's two a.m., let's get it going around six."

I groaned.

"Parker, you can do this," laughed Denny.

"But this is the time when I do my best work," I grumbled.

"You need sleep. Go, go get in your bed and I'll put Potus by your door. You'll be safe."

I rolled my eyes and did it anyway.

The last thing I saw were the ladies stretched out on the floor with blankets over them. The last thing I heard, in my bedroom with the door shut, was the ungodly sound of unladylike snoring.

Lord, give me mercy!

CHAPTER 35

Anne and Chauncey settled into the bed and breakfast and took a well-deserved and very much needed nap. Several hours later, they left their accommodations and headed down to the local pub.

Holding a pint in his hand, Chauncey nodded to Anne. "Three o'clock, same guy that was at the airport. Believe I'll have a word with him."

Anne shook her head. "Not yet. Do you really want to tip our hand that we're much more than bumbling old people traveling?"

Chauncey laughed. "My dear, that's one thing I've always loved about you. You have to remind me what we look like versus what we really are, or, I should really say, what we used to be."

Robert came through the door, glanced at them, slightly raising his eyebrows. Chauncey rolled his eyes to the right, barely nodded his head, and then shrugged ever so slightly.

Robert came over and slide in next to Anne. Waving his hand with one finger extended at the barkeep, he said, "Your fan club seem to be private hires from Paris."

Chauncey stroked his mustache a couple of times. The waitress plunked down Robert's beer.

"Anything else?"

"Not right now, thanks. Wait!"

The barmaid turned back around. "Yes?"

"Do you know the gentleman at the bar? The one with the brown jacket?"

She glanced over. "Him? Yeah. He fancies himself as a private detective. Some private investigator, if you ask me. He couldn't figure out who snatched his wife away from him until she married the bloke."

Anne laid a five-pound note on the table. "Thank you, dear."

The waitress picked it up with a practiced hand. "Would you like his business card on the sly?"

Anne smiled. "You are most accommodating, my dear."

Robert and Chauncey smiled. "You do have a way, my dear."

A few moments later, the waitress was back asking if they'd like another round. They nodded yes and she laid a business card next to Chauncey's beer. As Robert got up to go the loo, he picked up the card and slipped it into his pocket.

A few moments later he was back and they all had fresh beers.

"This guy probably couldn't find his way out of a plastic bag. He interviewed with Scotland Yard but after two interviews he washed out. He then tried to get on with MI5 and MI6, first interview which lasted less than thirty minutes with both of them, he then hung out his shingle saying he had trained with Scotland Yard.

"They found out about it and had a discussion with him. Now he says he has Scotland Yard contacts. He does predominantly divorce cases. How he came to tracking you, we're not sure but the call came in from Paris."

"That's interesting," said Chauncey nodding his head and raising his bushy white eyebrows. "I started to go speak with him or buy him a beer, but I think all he's supposed to do is see where we go and what we do, probably a report on who we speak to as well. He's probably harmless."

"Probably," agreed Robert, "but those guys that were following you earlier, they're serious. Be careful. We have you under surveillance, but we won't step in unless something untoward goes down."

"Thank you."

Robert tossed a ten-pound note on the table. "That ought to take care of most of it or leave it for the waitress. Nice to meet you. Enjoy your stay in London."

They both nodded.

"What say we go down to the little restaurant on the corner that we passed and have some dinner?" asked Anne.

"A splendid idea."

CHAPTER 36

I smelled coffee and...doughnuts? Had one of the girls snuck in during my precious four hours of sleep and inserted a Lady Gatorette doughnut gene in me? I cautiously crawled out from under the covers and looked to see if I had needle marks anywhere. Nope, I was safe...maybe.

Opening the bedroom door, I stepped over Potus into the living room. Misty Dawn barely glanced up from her computer. "You're not dressed appropriately. We're in the fourth quarter playing FSU. Where are your Gator colors?"

Oops. I hadn't paid much attention to the Reba McEntire tee shirt I had grabbed to go with my jeans. I went back into my bedroom and came out wearing a Gator polo shirt.

"Better."

Yeah, like we're all serious fashionistas here. Good news was all of the ladies were up and busy working on their laptops. Someone handed me a coffee mug and as soon as the nectar of the gods hit my taste buds I became somewhat alive again.

"Any news on anything?" I asked.

Everyone ignored me. I wandered into the kitchen when Rhonda Jean shouted, "The plain glazed doughnuts are mine."

Oh, heaven forbid, if I ate the wrong doughnut! I could feel a nasty retort trying to work itself out over the tongue and through the lips, but Denny stopped me before the words ever left my mouth.

"I need to talk to you." He held open the back door. Potus shot past me in a flash then stood in the middle of the back yard with his ears up and swiveling his head for intruders.

Sipping my coffee, I nodded at him. "So, what's up?"

"I got a call and the request is we drop research on Anne and Chauncey."

I was shocked. We may have stumbled into something way bigger than I ever dreamed possible.

"Do I dare ask why?"

"Parker, he and Anne both have Q clearances. Chains are being rattled and we're probably moving into areas we don't need to be in."

"Really, over a silly egg and some bureaucrat is getting his tighty whities in an uproar?" I sputtered. I reacted to Denny's comment versus responding.

"Parker, you, me, we don't know what else is at stake here. All I'm saying is one of the Gatorettes got into the government database, put in Anne and Chauncey's info and it set off bells and whistles."

Taking a deep breath, I had to admit I was impressed any of the girls could do that.

"Maybe I should hire whoever did that." I smirked.

He laughed, "Maybe so."

"Think we need to pull out?"

Denny thought for a moment and then shook his head. "No, I don't think so. You and I both already have Q clearances. All this really means for us is that big brother is going to be watching everything we do."

I snorted.

"Yeah, yeah, yeah, I know they watch everything anyway but as long as we're not interrupting national security in anyway, I don't think anyone's going to be that interested in us."

"Especially when they find out we're just chasing after a jeweled Easter egg." I smiled over the top of my mug.

Sigh, well, I've been wrong before.

CHAPTER 37

After an uneventful night, Anne and Chauncey went back to Heathrow and flew into Paris.

"You know she knows that we spent the night in London." More of a statement than a question.

Chauncey nodded. "Those first two weren't her guys tracking us, maybe Anatoly has some of his guys tracking her guys. Of course, that smacks of professionals or the government. We'll see what she has to say."

Arriving at Mathilde's older but very well-kept building, the doorman refused to let them enter until he had called her. Giving them the traditional look-down-your-nose-at-Americans look, he escorted them to the elevator, put his key into a lock next to the penthouse button, pushed it and then stepped out of the elevator.

Anne and Chauncey looked at each other and smiled.

The maid opened the opulent door and ushered them into Mathilde's sitting room. Chauncey looked around the room, taking it all in. Anne walked immediately over to Mathilde who was dressed all in white and gave her an air hug and kiss on both cheeks.

"So nice to see you again, Mathilde," she said smiling warmly.

Mathilde didn't acknowledge Anne. She was staring at Chauncey. He continued to gaze around the room.

Mathilde said coldly, "I see you finally made it here."

"This is the date on the tickets. I'm assuming you expected us today. If not," Chauncey shrugged, "we can come back tomorrow."

Her eyes were black, menacing and then softened. All a ruse, he knew. He had seen how she manipulated men before.

"Chauncey, Anne, come have a seat. Would you like some tea?"

In unison, they both said, "No, thank you."

She stared at them for a moment and then said, "Let's get on with it, shall we? How did you get the Royal Danish Fabergé Hen Egg?"

Chauncey sat in the ornate Russian chair with his legs crossed and his hands clasped. No response.

"You realize this egg was created for me?" she arched an elegantly sculptured eyebrow at him.

Chauncey smiled slightly. "There were fifty or maybe fifty-three eggs created, no one knows for sure. Out of the normally recognized fifty eggs, only forty-seven have been located.

"The Royal Danish Egg was created for Nicholas II to present to his mother, the Dowager Empress Maria Feodoraovana who escaped the Russian Revolution. She came to London and then went back to her native Denmark."

He leaned back in his chair, fingertips together. "So, no, the egg wasn't created for you, Mathilde. Nicholas may have showed it to you, but it was definitely created for his mother."

"Lies!" Mathilde shouted, standing. "I want that egg! Where is it?"

Anne was sitting very still, hands folded, watching her husband carefully.

He shifted slightly in his chair. "Mathilde, you need to call off your ruffians in Po'thole on the Lady Gatorettes and Parker Bell. They have nothing to do with us...or the egg. Trying to drown one of the girls is beyond what I thought you were capable of."

Mathilde sat back down. "Chauncey, you have no idea what I'm capable of. I have been through the Russian Revolution, I have survived in spite of numerous attempts to silence me. As to those American female idiots..."

"Mathilde," Anne spoke quietly. "They're not idiots. The people you hired are because they've been outwitted at every turn by them."

Chauncey looked at Anne, slightly nodding his head. "Mathilde, while you may think I'm the illegitimate son of Vova and you're my grandmother, nothing could be further from the truth. I was born in America and Vova is very definitely not my father."

Standing up, he said, "This meeting is over. Don't contact me again and," he paused, "call off your people on Anne, myself, and anyone in Po'thole."

Turning, he said, "Tell Anatoly the same thing."

"Or what?" Mathilde sneered. "I have nothing to do with that Russian peasant. Everything is always about money to him."

Chauncey held out his hand to Anne, helping her up from the chair. "Good day, Mathilde. We'll let ourselves out."

As they got to the door, Mathilde said, "It's not over, Chauncey. I want that egg!"

The door shut with a slight thwack.

CHAPTER 38

"Woot, woot!" shouted Rhonda Jean, jumping up from her chair. Everyone turned to look at her.

"Woot, woot, what?" asked Denny.

"I think I found the rabbit trail with Anne and Chauncey." Grinning, Rhonda Jean was doing the happy dance. I will be blinded for life with that vision.

Everyone had stopped what they were doing and turned to look at Rhonda Jean. She was still dancing, I don't know if I can bleach that from my memory.

"Okay, we know that Anne and Chauncey summer in Ellsworth and winter here, right?" Everyone nodded their heads.

"We know that they went to an antique show in Bangor." Again, more nodding of the heads.

"Well, here's where it gets really interesting. I decided to do a little more checking on Anne and Chauncey and their background is pretty interesting." More big grins and dance moves that will never be seen on national tv.

"Anne is a retired nurse and, according to social media, Chauncey is a professor of Advanced Avuncular Studies."

"Huh? What's that mean?" asked Myrtle Sue. Pretty much all of the other gals had a befuddled look on their faces as well.

"I had to look it up too," explained Rhonda Jean. "It means once a man reaches middle age and his formerly remarkable and youthful looks have completely lost their edge, he develops an air of such utter harmlessness that he is no longer attractive to women. It's when he stops looking like a sexual entity and starts looking like his Uncle Arby, according to the Urban Dictionary."

"So, Chauncey plays the part of the family uncle that everyone loves?" asked Flo, grinning and shaking her head.

"I guess. But, here's what's interesting, it appears that Chauncey hasn't had a job in years and years. Anne's the one who is the primary bread winner."

"What's up with that?" asked Misty Dawn. I could see the wheels spinning in her head and, goodness knows, they were certainly spinning in mine. Something wasn't adding up one hundred percent.

"How far back did you track Chauncey and Anne?" I asked. Something somewhere had to give us more information on them.

Clapping her hands happily, Rhonda Jean grinned. "Y'all ready? I think Anne and Chauncey may have been spies."

Gasps of "you're kidding," "seriously?" "not really, really?" were heard. Me? I think I zoned out for a moment because a lot of things were now starting to make sense.

"They were..."

"Hiding in plain sight for years," finished Denny. "The best defense is a good offense. It makes perfect sense. What's the rest of their backgrounds?"

"Chauncey graduated from the University of Maine in..." she paused.

"What?" everyone asked eagerly.

"Russian history."

Wow! Really?

"His master's degree was in..." she looked around the room, making sure we were all paying attention to her. "Russian art history."

I stood rooted to the floor. My mind was spinning like a whirling dervish. Things were starting to come together. There were gaps for sure, but some things were starting to add up.

Continuing on, Rhonda Jean, said, "The CIA recruited Chauncey right out of college and sent him to Vermont to learn Russian from some of the displaced counts from the Russian Revolution. They had escaped and, I'm guessing from what I've been able to find out, is that many of them came through Turkey to London and then to the U.S. where our government was more than happy to relocate them here, probably in exchange for information."

"Was, is, Chauncey a Russian spy?" asked Mary Jane.

"That I don't know. Maybe he was a double agent." She shrugged her shoulders. "Chauncey was on the government nickel for about a year and then taught one year of elementary school. He went back to Vermont for six months, presumably on the CIA's nickel, left them and hasn't worked a 'real' job since or, at least, I can't find evidence of one."

"What about Anne?" asked Denny.

"She went to nursing school, graduated as a R.N., met Chauncey in New York City, and they've been together ever since. But, once she graduated, she only took jobs that were out of the country.

"While Chauncey's fluent in Russian, Anne speaks multiple languages, Spanish, Cuban, French, and, possibly, some Russian."

Everyone was quiet for a moment, processing the information.

Then Denny said, "What makes you think they might have been spies though? Maybe they were just an adventurous couple who figured out how to travel the world, make some money, and have a good time. Others have done it."

"True," Rhonda Jean grinned some more, "but I found some memos that indicate they might have been making contacts or passing off things while they were out of the country."

Rut row! Now I know why Denny said we might be stepping into something bigger than what we originally thought. Although being cautious was never going to be my middle name, it did occur to me we might need to be a little bit more careful.

"And where did you find these memos?" asked Denny. He was half-smiling and looking at her.

"Um, maybe a database not available to the average public." Rhonda Jean was waffling a little.

"And how did you get access to this particular, I'm guessing, government database?"

"Um, the dark web?" She kind of rolled her eyes. "Or maybe there's a software program out there where you can access a number of different things."

Denny chuckled. "What made you look for Anne and Chauncey in a government database?"

"Once I realized what Chauncey's majors were and that he was hired by the CIA as a Russian art historian. Then when he quit, I figured there had to be a record of him somewhere.

"As you said, hiding in plain sight is the best way to throw off anyone looking for him or Anne. Guilty people, so to speak, don't usually hide in plain sight. They go to great lengths not to be seen. Anne and Chauncey, on the other hand, seem to be pretty cavalier about where they've been. It's a great offense."

I was impressed. I could tell Denny was impressed as well.

I said slowly, "You know, tapping into a government database is going to wave flags and let someone know that we've accessed files, don't you?"

"Yes, of course but what better way than to find out what's going?"

She did have a point.

"Besides," she grinned. "You're the one with the Q clearance, not me."

Great. I've been outflanked by a Lady Gatorette. I felt a headache coming on.

CHAPTER 39

"What do you think Mathilde is going to do, Chauncey?" asked Anne on the way down in the elevator.

"Follow us. She knows if we are harmed in any way, it's going to set off bells and whistles in certain circles. I'm sure she doesn't want that to occur because it would point back to her."

"Do think she'll hurt Parker and the girls? They've really been dragged into this thing totally without knowing a thing."

Chauncey chuckled as they exited the building. "True and look how well they've managed in spite of everything."

"I don't imagine they're going to take it very well the next time Mathilde's guys try to do something to them."

Chauncey smiled, "I don't imagine so. In fact, that's what I'm hoping for. Now, Anatoly's guys, on the other hand, that could be messy. But, my dear, I do have an idea that may alleviate a lot of problems for us, and the girls. Let's have dinner and let me tell you."

"I'm sure it will be brilliant," smiled Anne. "As always."

CHAPTER 40

"**I** found something," piped up Mary Jane. We all turned to look at her. I felt like the bobble-headed dog that sits in the back seat of some older cars.

"What?" I asked. I tried raising my eyebrows, but I think they were in the off position. I couldn't get them to move up or down.

"Vova, Mathilde's son, is supposedly British Intelligence working under the guise of being a translator and journalist. Although it is rumored he's gay, supposedly he may have had a love child at some point. And that love child is…"

"Chauncey!" Everyone shouted.

I felt my eyeballs rotating in their sockets. My brain cells felt like a ping pong ball was bouncing merrily back and forth between the opposite sides of my skull.

Mary Jane started to laugh. "Not true, though."

"Ohhh." Everyone moaned.

"Chauncey was born in America to American dad Fred Livingstone and English mom Lucy Clarke. Mom and Dad had moved to the U.S., actually to Maine, where Chauncey was born and then they divorced when he was around five. Fred was killed in a car accident shortly after the divorce."

More "awe's."

She continued on. "Mom actually knew Vova but there was no secret love tryst or affair between them. He was a friend of the family.

"After Fred died, Lucy worked as a secretary to support herself and Chauncey. She never remarried. She died when Chauncey was seventeen of..." a pregnant pause, "another car accident."

"I'm surprised if Chauncey ever drove a car based on family history." I said dryly. "I'd be very leery of his driving skills."

I was ignored.

"And we know the rest based on what Rhonda Jean found." Mary Jane bowed with a flourish and big grin.

"So, what's the deal with the egg?" asked Misty Dawn. "All of that other information is interesting, but it really doesn't tell us anything up to now. Specifically, how did Chauncey get the egg? Is it truly an original Fabergé or a fake? Why is this Mathilde interested in it? Why is this Anatoly Petrov over the edge about it? And, more importantly, why are these people so ready to kill for it? Specifically, why are they so ready to kill me and my girls?" She looked sheepishly at me. "And Gracie Blanche."

"I'm guessing it's not only because of the historical aspect of it but because it's one of the missing Fabergé eggs," said Denny. "However, I really think it has more to do with a personal connection to the egg. Mathilde, Anatoly, and Chauncey all have some personal connection to the egg. I think that's what we need to focus on. What's the personal connection for each one of these people? When we find that out, then the real answers will show up."

"Who's working on the Mathilde connection?" I asked.

"Me," answered Myrtle Sue. Clearing her throat, she said, "I can't really find proof of this but I'm guessing Mathilde thinks the egg is for her. Based on the timeframe, the egg couldn't have been created for her because it was for the Dowager Empress, Nicholas' mother. Since Mathilde was a courtesan and shared her body with at least three of the royal family that we know of, I'm guessing someone told her the egg was hers. Maybe to impress her, if nothing else.

"I'm also guessing that the egg wasn't high on her mind when she escaped the Russian Revolution and moved to Paris. That probably didn't surface until many years later."

Myrtle Sue shrugged. "Maybe she got into a fight with her husband, Count Andrei, and asked where it was. Who knows?

"Since Vova is allegedly British Intelligence, I'm guessing he was never that interested in the egg or its location or he would have been looking for it since he has a lot of resources at his fingertips.

"Now that she's older, maybe she wants it back to remind her of her glory days or maybe she wants to sell it and make a bundle from it. As one of the lost eggs, I'm guessing the price would be very high if it were sold."

Denny and I nodded. All of that made sense.

"Other than me, who else is working on the Anatoly connection?" I looked around at them.

"Me," said Misty Dawn. "I'd also like to go on record at this point and say the next whackos that come after any of us are going to be swimming in the St. Johns River with anchors tied to their feet. No more being nice. If they're going to try to kill us, any of us, then they need to expect their lives to be cut short."

The Lady Gatorettes nodded their heads in unison. Denny poked me because I was nodding my head up and down as well.

"What?" I asked angrily. "If those bozos are trying to kill me, Gracie Blanche, you, or the girls, then they can become fish food for all I care."

Denny's eyes narrowed. "Just you don't do it, let one of us do it."

Well, yeah, there's that factor. These folks know how to kill. Me? I've only watched how to do it in the movies.

Misty Dawn said, "Based on the information that Andrew and Missy gave us, I can't be sure, but I think Anatoly's dad might have been a servant or low-level guard-type person who accompanied some of the Russian nobility out of Russia and into the U.S."

She groaned, "These people changed up their last names constantly, particularly once they got out of Russia, and it's kind of hard to figure out who was traveling with whom.

"I think Anatoly's dad came to the U.S. and ended up in Vermont."

"Whoa!" shouted Flo. "Is this Anatoly guy actually an American? That would be wild!"

"No, no," said Misty Dawn. "He was definitely born in Russia. I think his dad came here first and then when his Count died he went back to Russia which is where Anatoly was born."

"So, did he bring the egg with him or, rather, did this Count guy bring the egg and use it as a bargaining tool to get into the U.S.?" Denny's eyes shone brightly with anticipation of newly discovered information.

"Not sure," answered Misty Dawn, "but here's what I do know. Chauncey learned Russian from these guys in Vermont and maybe the egg was given to Chauncey for safe-keeping. Remember, Chauncey was working for the CIA at this point and, maybe, just maybe, no one really cared about this egg and maybe, just maybe, the egg disappeared.

"Also, remember, these eggs didn't become a big deal until about the last twenty or thirty years. Chauncey may have helped a Count or his family out and the egg was used as payment.

"As a Russian Art History major, Chauncey would probably have been more than thrilled to have an original Fabergé egg, and that's what I'm betting happened. He would also know the true value of an egg like this."

Denny scratched his head. "So maybe Anatoly thinks the egg really should be his since, or if, his dad took care of a Count. As a loyal Russian, I can see where an American getting the egg would fry his goat."

He shook his head back and forth thinking out loud. "Not only would this be personal to him as a Russian but also in thinking that the egg was stolen or taken from his dad. That would definitely make sense, especially based on his conversation with you, Parker."

"Yes, it does," I said. "I'm wondering though if this egg could be used to manipulate any of the international money markets. I'm basing this on what Andrew said."

"Doesn't make sense," flatly stated Misty Dawn. "The egg probably isn't worth more than fifty million dollars tops and I don't think that's enough to manipulate international money markets."

"Really?" I gasped in surprise. These girls' knowledge extended way past the boundaries of Po'thole. I was definitely impressed.

"What? I watch Jim Cramer's Mad Money show." She grinned wickedly. "It is, however, enough to rock the art history world and what would make a bigger splash than a Russian billionaire finding a lost Fabergé egg? His stock could definitely go up."

We all looked at each other and smiled.

"However, I still want to kill those bozos who tried to drown me."

CHAPTER 41

"Why, Chauncey, I do believe that's a splendid idea! Do you think we need to tell Parker and her friends the plan?" Anne was almost giddy with relief. "Maybe Anatoly and Mathilde will call off their goons."

Chauncey smiled. "I think we should tell them but after everything is set up and the egg has changed hands. There will be no reason to hurt anyone after the egg has been delivered."

"My dear, I do think this is your best idea ever." She smiled lovingly at her husband. "And, then maybe next time you won't have your picture taken at any antique show."

They both laughed.

CHAPTER 42

We had decided to wait on making our information public until Anne and Chauncey had returned to Po'thole. Ironically enough, Chauncey called me a couple of hours after the girls and I had the brainstorming pow wow at my house. He said he and Anne would be back in town by the weekend and they would explain everything to us regarding the Fabergé Easter Egg.

As I was thinking back on his conversation, my cell phone rang with an international number.

"Parker Bell here."

"Ms. Bell, this is Anatoly Petrov."

Well, this certainly was a surprise. I was a little cautious for several reasons, the very least of which I wanted to make sure I wasn't getting ready to be killed. I pulled the curtains back slightly in the living room to see if I spotted any unwelcome guests, but my yard was empty.

"Yes, Mr. Petrov. To what do I owe this pleasure?" My tone was even.

"I just wanted to let you know that you will not have to worry about anything from me."

I pulled my phone away from my ear and looked at it.

"Does that include all of my friends as well?" This whole conversation was bordering on being a little odd. It was a read-between-the-lines conversation. It was almost like we were telling each other life was going to be good again.

"Yes. If anything else occurs, it is not from me. Also," he paused, "nothing, other than my phone calls to you, was ever from me."

"Mr. Petrov, I'm curious. Who were the visits from then?" I held my breath hoping he would provide an answer. In all honesty, I wasn't sure if I would even believe him. Of course, it depended upon his answer.

Then was a long pause, then, "Perhaps someone from France sent multiple visitors to you and perhaps this person was trying to manipulate me as well. Good day, Ms. Bell."

I looked at my cell phone. I still wasn't sure about a lot of things but having Anatoly off my back was a big relief. Apparently, he no longer had a dog in this race.

Saturday morning, all of the Lady Gatoretes, Denny, Anne and Chauncey were at my house. The air was permeated with coffee and doughnut aromas. I inwardly sighed when I saw the five boxes of various flavors of doughnuts sitting on my dining room table. There were only nine people but sixty doughnuts. I shuddered and hoped none of the girls were going to go crazy with all of the sugar and caffeine.

Chauncey winked at me as he finished up his second doughnut.

"Alright, alright," I shouted. "Chauncey's wanting to tell us what's going on."

Chauncey said, "Why don't you tell me what you know and then I'll fill you in on the rest."

I nodded at Denny and he reported everything that we knew.

Anne and Chauncey looked at each with a slightly bemused look on their faces.

"What does that look mean?" asked Rhonda Jean. "I've only seen that look when the Gator coaches know their players are better than the other team, but the other team hasn't discovered that yet."

"All of you are very smart, smarter than what you've been given credit for," murmured Anne smiling.

Everyone grinned and high fived each other.

"You pretty much guessed everything." Chauncey looked around the room with a slight grin. "There's been enough physical violence and it's ending now.

I am selling the Fabergé egg to Anatoly Petrov and it will make the news on Monday."

Everyone started chattering at once.

"Wait, wait!" Chauncey's smile became even bigger as he held up his hand. "Here's how we're having it presented. A lady will have discovered the egg in a warehouse while going through a deceased relative's things. She contacts Parker because she has read all of her true crime books and thinks Parker can help her do the right thing with this egg. She's not even sure the egg is of any real value but knows it's very pretty.

"Ironically enough, Parker has been doing research on various lost art treasures for her next book and recognizes the egg as the lost Royal Danish Fabergé Egg.

"Because of Parker's various connections around the world, she is aware Anatoly collects Fabergé eggs and knows he wants them all to be returned to Russia. He wants the eggs returned so the Russian people can enjoy viewing their royal heritage."

"I what?!" I almost became completely unglued. "This is nuts!"

"Oh, it gets better, Parker," grinned Chauncey. Anne also smiled with a twinkle in her eye as she sipped her tea.

"You will be promoted as a very successful international author, we're leaving out that you also own a computer security business, and your book sales will probably go way up because of this.

"Anyway, you know how much goodwill this will generate between our two countries. You convince this anonymous lady to extend a hand-across-the-water and generously donate this royal egg back to its home country where the Russian people can view it in Anatoly's museum. It will be announced on the national television news on Monday."

"You mean you're going to sell or give your egg to Petrov to stop all of this craziness?" Misty Dawn asked doubtfully.

"Yes, we're selling the egg but that won't be disclosed. The good news is you won't have to worry about any more thugs."

"Unless they're from this Mathilde person," said Myrtle Sue and winked. "If they bother us again, you probably won't hear from them ever again in this lifetime."

"One question." I held up my hand. "Why does, did, everyone think I knew where the egg was?"

Anne answered, "Oh, my dear, that's easy."

I cocked my head.

"It's because you write those true crime novels and you help solve cases. What better person to help solve where a lost Fabergé Easter Egg might be?"

Well, she might have a point on that.

"Are you and Anne really spies?" asked Flo.

Anne and Chauncey just laughed.

CHAPTER 43

T his was a big moment being on national television and meeting Anatoly at the same time and I was a little nervous.

It was impressive as Anatoly unveiled the precious Fabergé egg to the world. It had been in a plain, non-descript box for some thirty years, according to the television anchor, and I nodded yes. It was being hailed as a major art find, one that would keep the art historians busy for years trying to trace its origin.

Denny told me later than all of the girls had whooped and hollered when they saw me on the big screen tv at my house. He assured me the house was still in one piece and that it was clean.

In spite of what was being told on tv and in the newspapers, how did we actually manage to piece all of the details together before Anne and Chauncey filled us in with the few remaining details we didn't know? Luck, and the fact that Rhonda Jean had tapped into the unauthorized government database. We obviously didn't have all of the details, but we were able to piece everything together by sheer determination and logic. It was like putting together a big puzzle.

Five minutes after I returned home...oops, Po'thole...Denny received a phone call and he took it outside because the Lady Gatorettes were noisily celebrating my return. Yes, they had all gathered, once again, at my house. A few minutes later, he came back inside and wiggled his finger for me to go out with him.

I raised my eyebrows, finally they went up, and I went outside with him.

"Unofficially, we did good," he grinned. "But, officially, we can't tap into the database anymore without our Q clearances being revoked. You and I both need those clearances. Do you think Rhonda Jean would do that again on a just because basis?"

I thought for a moment and then shook my head. "Doubtful, she's gotten the info she wanted." I grinned, "Besides SEC football season is coming up and that's all she cares about."

We laughed. Life was good.

CHAPTER 44

Anne and Chauncey watched Anatoly's announcement from their little color television with the rabbit ears. Reception was okay but since they rarely watched tv they didn't care.

"When do you think he'll notice?" asked Anne with a mischievous grin.

"Probably never," answered Chauncey. "Other than us, everyone else is dead. Mathilde will soon know Anatoly has it and there's absolutely no reason for her to come after us for any reason. Plus, she's not going to spend any more money on something that she can't have. Anatoly certainly isn't going to give it to her."

"Was the money transferred into our Grand Cayman account?"

"Yes, Anne, it was. Then it was transferred to Germany and then to Switzerland. It's safe and we have plenty of money for the rest of our lives."

He gently lifted out the exquisitely beautiful Royal Danish Fabergé Easter egg out of its very ornate box and set it on their country French dining table.

"There are no records that still exist that show two eggs were made. The real one was made by Carl Fabergé in St. Petersburg and his name is written in Cyrillic on the egg. This is the one that was made for the Dowager Empress." He gently opened the egg and showed Anne.

"The other egg was made in Moscow by one of his other designers and not all of those jewels are of the same quality as our egg."

They looked at each other with love and smiled.

"My dear, you are brilliant."

"Why, thank you, Anne," said Chauncey with his eyes twinkling.

CHAPTER 45

"Gracie Blanche, I swear I never even saw Anne and Chauncey's egg until I was on tv!" I was exasperated, and I was rolling my eyes at the phone. There was a lot of chattering on the phone.

"Gracie Blanche, Gracie Blanche, GRACIE BLANCHE!" I shouted into the phone. "Please stop!"

I heard a muffled voice on the other end of my phone. "If you're cursing at me, let me just point out while you've been laying around and being waited on twenty-four, seven, I've been out there solving..."

Being interrupted for the third time in less than fifteen minutes was causing my temper to erupt. It didn't make any difference how lousy Gracie Blanche might feel, she could at least listen to me.

"What? Yeah, okay, I'll see you at three."

Denny was laying on my couch and laughed. "Everything's back to normal with you two."

I shrugged and sort of laughed. "I guess."

"Did you tell her you're giving serious thought to moving back here?"

I groaned and shook my head.

"You know that would probably make her day, don't you, Parker?"

"Probably except I don't want to help her with any of those crappy antique shows she does."

Denny laughed again.

My phone rang and without looking at caller ID, I must be slipping, I answered it.

"Parker, darling, I thought you were going to call me with your new book idea."

God hates me, He really does.

"Saffron, there's really not a whole lot to tell. No book deal this time." I said wearily.

"Parker, honey, I saw you on tv. There is a marvelous opportunity to capitalize on the popularity of this Fabergé Easter Egg." She paused, "Plus, I do believe I heard you were working on another book."

She sniffed, "And to think you didn't even tell your book agent extraordinaire that's what you were working on. I had to find it out on the Today show."

I rolled my eyes but she couldn't see them.

Her tone hardened. "Parker, honey, I've already gotten you a book deal. So I need to see the outline by the end of next week. I think we can have it ready in time for Christmas. Ciao, sweetness."

I sat down on the couch with my head between my hands. Denny was still standing, grinning.

"I'm guessing Saffron just got another major book deal for you and I'm guessing you need to start writing it."

I nodded my head ever so slightly.

CHAPTER 46

L ove her, hate her, Saffron worked her magic and got me the biggest advance in the history of my publishing company, and pre-orders of the book were off the charts.

Sitting in front of abnormally hot television studio lights, host Paula Hotten lead off the interview with, "Parker, tell me how you came find one of the lost Fabergé eggs."

I smiled demurely. "Paula, truth is stranger than fiction. It is truly an unbelievable story."

Discover more of Parker Bell and those crazy Lady Gatorettes. Flip the page and read the first chapter of *Little Candy Hearts and Murder*.

Thank you so much for reading *The Faberge Easter Egg and Murder*. Authors love...and need...reviews. I would greatly appreciate it!

I know you want some giggles and grins because, let's face it, life can be pretty miserable without a bit of humor. Click here to sign up for my twice-a-month newsletter. PLUS, you'll receive a free book. Woo hoo!

LITTLE CANDY HEARTS

LITTLE CANDY HEARTS

"What do you mean has the love bandit struck?" I was dumbfounded and, yes, I rolled my eyes at the possibility someone had a romantic interest in me in this little quaint, redneck town where I was currently residing. I did hold a desire in my heart to move back to Atlanta but, unfortunately, this crazy small town had me on a Velcro leash and I could only run so far before it snapped me back like a nasty bungee cord.

"Has Joe D. gotten divorced again?" I could feel a headache coming on. Since I was standing in the pristine kitchen of my relatively new modular home sipping on some nectar of the gods better known as Ecuador's finest coffee, I wasn't sure what Gracie Blanche, my oldest friend since fourth grade, was alluding to.

I could already tell this was going to be one of those days where I was sorry I had even rolled out of bed...literally. For some reason, my feet never wanted to land on the floor when getting out of bed. Instead, I had a nasty habit of actually rolling out of the bed and landing on the floor on my fanny.

I blamed it on the fact that I was never fully awake until I had at least one cup of coffee. Don't even bother suggesting I put an automatic coffee maker on the nightstand. I tried that and ended up with coffee everywhere...on the floor, on me in bed, and, of course, all over the night table. It's not fun cleaning up a liquid mess first thing in the morning, particularly since I couldn't blame it on anyone else.

There was a giggle on the other end of the phone. "Parker, don't you know anything that is going on in town?"

Well, no, actually I don't. I wasn't prone to wandering the decaying streets of Po'thole, I hadn't lived here in umpteen years before the above said Velcro band snatched me back, and I didn't shop downtown where there was enough gossip amongst the storeowners to run almost anyone out of town. Once a rumor got started, true or not, it took on an exuberant life of its own.

Small town living wasn't for the faint of heart, especially if you had had the audacity to move away from here, which I had.

Since I had grown up here, left for a number of years, and then had been reluctantly dragged back to town to help Gracie Blanche with a couple of her antique shows. I had unfortunately been involved with solving several murders while vacationing here. I was past reasonably sure I have been the subject of many a store owner and their patrons' conversations. I wasn't willing to add fuel to their fire regarding me and I wasn't interested in destroying another individual's reputation.

"Gracie Blanche, I'm in the process of getting ready to go back to Atlanta. The city where I own my own company, remember, where people like me and don't try to kill me. Well, other than driving, but that doesn't count." I sighed because I knew nothing good was going to come from my next question. "Who or what is the love bandit and what does he have to do with me?"

"There's someone who is leaving little candy hearts on different women's vehicles at night." Gracie Blanche actually giggled. Let me point out, my four foot eleven inch friend is actually a modern day version of Attila the Hun. She has a very short fuse, particularly with me because I maintain she doesn't have a sense of humor, and she also has a wicked temper. Again, usually directed at me. To hear her giggle was almost un-nerving. Her laugh was something along the lines of a delighted pig at an all you can eat corn trough. Giggle was not a word that I had ever used to describe the humorous sound coming out of Gracie Blanche's mouth, but it was definitely a giggle and not her normal snorting sound.

"Parker, just look out your living room window and tell me if there is a box of little candy hearts on your windshield."

Only because it was mid-morning and I hadn't decided on what I was going to do for the day yet, I decided to humor her and padded over to my living room window to peer out. The fake hardwood floor was cold on my naked feet. The sun was out, the sky was blue, and, apparently, I had captured the heart of the so-called love bandit because spray painted all over my SUV was "Tweet Me, Just Saying, Insta Mine, Yolo, Let's Chill" and that's just what I could see from my window.

"Are you flipping kidding me?" I screamed. Yeah, well, Gracie Blanche isn't the only one in the universe with a short fuse. Seeing my new white SUV spray painted caused me to shout some words that should never be used around a daycare center or a ladies church group.

The more disturbing issue was I also sloshed some of my precious coffee on my new brown leather recliner next to the window. Good news was I could wipe it up. Bad news was I wasn't sure if I had any paper towels in the house. Regular terrycloth towels, yes; paper, probably not. I did not keep a well-stocked kitchen which is the reason why it's pristine. Other than always having coffee on hand, my refrigerator was painfully empty. As a single gal, I ate out a lot. Plus, I flunked home economics or whatever they called that cooking class that was a requirement for boys and girls in junior high school. If I can't stick it in the microwave and eat it, what's the point? It was far easier for me to run by a fast-food place and do a slide and glide. Martha Stewart I am not.

Gracie Blanche's voice went from teasing to concern in a nano-second. "Parker, what happened? Are you okay? Parker? Parker?"

"Gracie Blanche, if this is one of your jokes, I am not happy!" I shouted at her. "You, or someone, spray painted sayings all over my SUV. Really? You had to do that?"

I was literally almost foaming at the mouth I was so mad.

"Wha...what?" stammered Gracie Blanche. "No, Parker, I didn't do anything to your car."

Grinding my teeth, I managed to growl out, "I am not amused. That had better wash off easily. Who is this love bandit because I'm going to kill him!"

"Parker, I'll try to find out. Seriously," she paused, sounding a little subdued. "No one else has had this happened. Everybody else just had a box of little candy hearts left on their windshield."

Of course not! I'm some kind of special in this little, no-nothing town that refuses to let me live in Atlanta. WHERE I AM HAPPY! I ran my hand through my hair, frustrated. My hair is short and my running my hand through it gives it the appearance of a raccoon on a bad hair day. Why did Po'thole's unique brand of craziness attach itself to me like white on rice?

Let me back up for a redneck second and introduce myself to you. I'm Parker Bell, owner of a cyber security consulting firm and national bestselling crime author. I live in Atlanta, although you'd never know it considering how often I keep getting dragged back to Po'thole recently. Let me just say, being loyal to friends isn't all it's cracked up to be.

Po'thole, Florida, according to the chamber of commerce, is pronounced Poat, like goat, hole. The natives call it Po Ho and anyone north of Georgia calls it Pot Hole. Yes, even national television news anchors mispronounce the name. One would think they might actually do some research on how to pronounce names. Apparently, that requires too much work on their part. So much for confidence in news reporters.

I escaped the confines of this rural, economically depressed, and limited thinking little town located on the beautiful St. Johns River in Northeast Florida to the large metropolis of Atlanta, I created a very successful cyber security consulting company. Believing that both sides of my brain needed to be balanced and because I was getting bored with computer work, I started writing true crime novels. No one was more surprised than I was when my books became New York Times bestsellers.

I'm in my mid-thirties...or maybe a year or two older...I'm not particularly vain about my looks, although I do have my moments. I'm the height of your average female, five foot four inches to those of you not in the know. I can be somewhat sarcastic at times. Okay, most of the time, but I do try, sorta, to keep my mouth under control. Sigh, it's pretty much a losing battle.

Of course, once I see a conversation is heading south, it's irrelevant to me what I say. Which, cough, cough, has been known to get me in trouble. I personally think it's one of my more endearing qualities that I say what's true and on my mind. Unfortunately, a lot of people, including friends, don't agree with my assessment. I have been called smarty pants on a number of occasions. Alright, since I'm being honest and transparent, it's another variation on smarty pants and since I'm trying really hard to clean up my language, I'll leave it up to your imagination.

I have baby fine brown hair that refuses to conform to any type of beauty treatment, better known as I gave up on trying to do anything with it, and it's straight as a board...unless I don't run a comb through it after a shower and then it looks like I've stuck my finger in an electrical outlet. Oh, yeah, I have brown eyes, not those cute puppy dog eyes. I have had police officers tell me that I'm giving them the stink eye look when all I've been doing is looking at them while they are writing out a speeding ticket and wondering why more intelligent people don't go into law enforcement.

I'm single because those internet dating websites can't seem to find me a guy who is intelligent, has a sense of humor, and can breathe at the same time. I've been told I'm too picky. I would call it discerning. Whatever you call it, I'm now up to not being able to find a man within five hundred miles that I want to date.

Joe D. Savannah, owner of We Make Money CPAs, was my first love boy waaay back in the day and is currently on wife number three. He maintains the only reason why he keeps getting married and divorced is because I won't marry him.

He didn't want to leave Po'thole and go with me to Atlanta and I didn't want to live the rest of my life in this godforsaken little backwoods town. Although, sad to say and much to my chagrin, I'm sorta, maybe, cough, cough, thinking about possibly moving back here.

My cyber security business is to the point where it can pretty much run by itself and I have some really good managers in place. There's an advantage to planning ahead, although when I'm down here I can't seem to figure out how to do it. I think it's something in the air I'm breathing or...maybe it's in the water I'm drinking.

Crazy seems to not only follow me when I'm here but it attaches itself to me like Velcro being dragged through a sticker field. I can't seem to be left alone for any length of time without mayhem wanting to seriously date me or get married.

Oh, did I mention that dead bodies seem to magically find their way to me? I'm honestly surprised the FBI doesn't have my picture posted somewhere saying, "WARNING! Parker Bell is known to be a deterrent to living persons."

I am seriously thinking of killing this so-called love bandit if I can find him. The other dead bodies were because I was in close proximity to them. Okay, they were murdered but I did not do it. Things have a way of happening in Po'thole. I'd blame it on my perfume, but I don't wear any.

Pink's "So What" song started playing merrily on my cell phone interrupting my wandering thoughts. I glanced at the caller ID and groaned.

"Gracie Blanche, I'm going to have to call you back but you'd better find out who is doing this to my car." I pushed the off button on my cell phone before Gracie Blanche had a chance to respond.

"Hello."

"Parker, it's Rhonda Jean. Misty Dawn says we need to have a meeting at your house."

I rolled my eyes. "Is there a reason to do this?"

A slight pause. "Parker, it's Misty Dawn."

"Yes, Rhonda Jean, I get that but why do we need to have a meeting and at my house? What's up?" I was somewhat annoyed, although I knew I was in a losing battle. The Lady Gatorettes would show up at my house, invited or not, whenever they felt like it. Them actually asking if they could come over was a major improvement, which only heightened my curiosity level and also caused my stomach to start producing copious amounts of acid.

I walked back into my kitchen trying to remember if I had put the antacids in the bathroom or if they were hiding somewhere in a kitchen cabinet I was barely familiar with.

"Misty Dawn says we need to have a meeting about who spray painted your SUV."

Getting information out of Rhonda Jean was like pulling carrots up out of the ground. It was tough. However, she had found and hit my hot button.

"Do you know who did this to my car?" I shouted into the phone. "Plus, how did you know my SUV has been painted?"

"We'll see you in an hour." And that ended our conversation.

I probably should introduce you to the Lady Gatorettes. Some townspeople refer to them as Po'thole's version of the mafia. This would be incorrect.

The hormonally challenged, sugar-and-caffeine infused Lady Gatorettes – Mary Jane, Flo, Rhonda Jean, Myrtle Sue, and Misty Dawn – are a non-sanctioned division of the local University of Florida football booster club. The reason why they are non-sanctioned is because they got into a small altercation, okay the cops were called, many years ago and the powers that be in that club, yes everyone, decided the girls were not of the 'caliber' of members they wanted.

I will say it loud and hope that I can disavow ever saying these words in public, but the girls are just good plain old country girls and the term 'redneck' could be safely used on them. Professionals, such as those found in the booster club, do not appreciate some of God's more colorful characters in life.

The Lady Gatorettes are five hormonal women and have been best friends since elementary school. Unfortunately, they wreak havoc everywhere they go. Believing that caffeine and sugar are an important daily ritual and a major food group requirement, they consume more than their fair share. People cringe and leave establishments when they enter. I even quake in my sneakers sometimes. You just never know what these gals are going to do...even if they like you.

Here's the short rundown on these gals.

Flo is a tall, slim waitress with long out-of-the-bottle blond hair and brown eyes who is now on her sixth husband and makes one mean strawberry pie. Flo's reason for having so many husbands was because not one of them appreciated and loved the Gators as much as she did.

"Humph," she sniffs. "If my husband doesn't have a clue as to who the quarterback is, what type of offense the Gators are running, and who the coaches are, then what good is he to me?"

She also only dates men when it is not football season and that probably explains why she's never noticed that's why they knew nothing about Gator football. The ladies do not want company, including their husbands, bothering them on Saturday game day from September to the end of November, which explains why Flo only dates during the off-season.

Mary Jane, a very attractive brunette with puppy dog brown eyes from way back when, went to Atlanta for a weekend with some out-of-town cousins upon graduating from high school and since her return has never seemed quite right. There has been much speculation that she indulged in some cheap street pharmaceuticals and that is the reason why she sometimes twitches at odd times. No one knows for sure—she's never explained—and her out-of-town cousins disavow knowledge of anything. They also have never visited her ever again.

Apparently not realizing New York City is bigger than Atlanta and has more than its fair share of craziness, she moved there for a brief moment in time. She thought she was in love with the city that never sleeps at night, and allegedly she didn't sleep much either, changed her mind after a year, and came back. She's still a redneck but now has an educated palate. She also dates guys she meets on dating websites on the Internet. While the rest of the Lady Gatorettes occasionally scold her for surfing for men on the Internet, they are all secretly envious of her.

She also keeps track of Joe D. Savannah's latest profile on dating sites. His latest profile always creates a great deal of merriment amongst the girls when she finds a new one. She refuses to admit to being a stalker. Her version is she wants to make sure she doesn't show up on his "you might be a match" notification list.

Myrtle Sue, a little dark-haired fireplug of a woman, is a domestic goddess. She knows every recipe that has ever been on the Food Network. She also surfs the Internet constantly looking for new information and statistics on the Gators. Her husband, while not understanding a single thing about the Gator football team and could care less, worships the ground his wife walks on. As long as he gets at least one hot meal a day he's a happy camper. He also has been known to brag that Myrtle Sue makes the best sandwiches that can be eaten with one hand while driving his tractor out in the potato and cabbage fields.

Don't under-estimate Myrtle Sue's temper. She might look calm but there's a little volcano hiding inside that can erupt at any moment. J.W., her husband, discovered that the hard way.

During hunting season, Southern boys don't believe it's necessary to ask their wives for permission to go hunting or explain why they go off in the woods with other men getting sweaty, nasty, stinky, dirty, and still don't have a dead animal to show for what they were doing over the weekend.

Apparently, it was that time of the month for Myrtle Sue. She had come home from a particularly bad time at Wal-Mart and discovered that her husband had gone off for the weekend with the boys while leaving her a note saying he would see her Monday morning before he went to work. J.W. made the fatal error of telling her that he needed clean clothes for Monday.

Myrtle Sue saw red. She vowed that J.W. wouldn't have clean clothes for the remainder of hunting season because he'd made the fatal error of not saying "I love you" on his note.

After becoming a graduate of the 90-day Myrtle Sue School of Doing Your Own Laundry, J.W. now leaves notes with a great big "I Love You" on them. Marital bliss made its way back to the happy couple.

Rhonda Jean is the largest of the girls. She believes there is just more of her to love. She's not p-h-a-t, she just has a few extra pounds that have decided to stay with her...permanently. She is the trick play master. She knows every trick play that has been in a Gator game for the past thirty-five years. She also annoys the heck out of the coaches at Florida because she creates and sends in new trick plays every week during spring practice and the regular season.

When a new coach is hired, Rhonda Jean sends him every play that she has ever devised. Her fervent wish is that one of her plays will be used during a televised game and the Gators will run it in for a touchdown. So far it hasn't happened.

Her husband, Big T, short for Thomas the Third, is pleased as a pig in mud and mighty proud of his wife every time she receives a letter from the coaches. The fact that they are form letters doesn't bother him a bit. He just knows that one day one of his wife's plays will be used and then they will both be national celebrities.

Big T gave up chewing tobacco for dipping because dipping doesn't turn your teeth as brown and he's very proud of his big smile.

Misty Dawn, the ringleader of this happy little group, stays in the Lady Gatorettes version of the Witness Protection Program aka WPP pronounced WIP, because local law enforcement still thinks she's killed up to six men. Let me point out that she's been cleared of all those charges by the FBI but apparently that's not good enough for the River County sheriff Dewitt Munster, yes that's really his name, and he's a TV-Barney Fife look alike. He wants to put her in jail so badly that he's been known to run a red light or two thinking he's spotted her. She's still roaming around freely and waves at him when she sees him going in the opposite direction. It drives him crazy.

Misty Dawn was so named because that's what the morning looked like the day she was born, and her mother took that as a naming sign. She sends encouraging cards and notes to all of the football players who play in each game. She was tickled pink when one of the players mentioned on national TV that it was her cards and letters that helped him during the difficult ordeal of his brother being arrested for dog fighting.

Misty Dawn, unfortunately, isn't quite as dainty as what her name might indicate. Her swearing can put a military man to shame. Let me be fair and say, she's never said any horrendously bad words in front of me; however, the woman carries grudges like Christians forgive sins.

It's too bad that Misty Dawn didn't join the Navy. Swift, silent, and deadly, she would've made a natural Navy SEAL.

Her husband John Boy works construction and is afraid of no one except for his wife; however, he absolutely quivers when she walks in the house when she has that death-to-the-world glint in her eye.

If he doesn't let her vent when she gets mad, she goes out to the chicken house and they end up eating chicken for a month. Her record for killing chickens when she's in a state of anger is fifteen.

Sure enough, around noon, the girls burst through my front door laughing and carrying on. The good news was they brought lunch. The bad news was it was one pizza per person plus one extra. I knew sharing pizza was not something any of them did well. The last time they had tried to share pizza here at my house it resembled something out of the movie *Animal House*.

"Parker, there's something wrong here. You need to fix it now!" While Flo's mouth was smiling, her eyes were doing a borderline death stare. I glanced down and realized my major faux pas. Dashing into the bedroom and out again before anyone could shout "Go Gators!" I changed into the requisite orange and blue Gator shirt.

The girls all looked at each other, nodded, and grinned.

"Um, God, bless this food. Go ahead and dig in." Although I had not provided the pizza, they did have the courtesy to wait until I said a tiny little prayer of thanksgiving. Although the Lady Gatorettes were a wee bit on the rough side, they were very respectful when it came to prayer.

After a few minutes of listening to them eat, a vision of pigs eating at a trough waffled through my brain, Misty Dawn took a big swallow of Coke. Anything that is carbonated in the South is a Coke, it doesn't make any difference what the brand name is, it's always a Coke and it's always a real Coke with the Lady Gatorettes.

"Parker, John Boy drove past your house this morning on the way to work and saw that your SUV had been spray painted with day-glow paint," she said.

"What?!" I hadn't even noticed that the paint was day glow colors. The only thing I had noticed was my vehicle was covered in childish Valentine's Day sayings.

"Yep. He said you probably could be seen an easy half mile away if you were driving when it was dark."

Although there were a few slight chuckles and a rolling of the eyes, no one broke out in raucous laughter. Probably because my face had gone beet red and I was taking deep breaths. I put my never empty coffee cup on the table. That was a true indication of how upset I was.

Mary Jane, bless her heart – not always a term of endearment in the South, it has approximately one hundred sixty meanings and it depends totally on the tonal inflection as to the specific meaning. If you're not from the South, you're never going to understand the true meaning...you might get close, but you won't understand the specific meaning.

Anyway, Mary Jane had taken some yoga classes way back and knew some deep breathing exercises to allegedly calm the body and soul. She had tried to show me on several occasions. I wasn't interested. I mean, after all, what's the point of a good snit if you can't blow up?

"Who did this to my vehicle?" I managed to growl out.

They all looked at each other and shook their heads.

"Well, I've heard rumors," Misty Dawn looked around the table and nodded at the girls. "They have too. Someone is leaving those little candy hearts at various women's homes or in their mailbox."

Flo broke in, grinning, looking around, bouncing her head up and down. "That, of course, is against federal regulations according to the post office."

I took a deep breath. I felt like they knew something but were unwilling to share it with me. This was like pulling teeth out of a donkey's mouth.

"Is Joe D. looking for another wife and this is his way of seeing who's interested?" If it was Joe D., then he had fallen to new lows. Although, in all honesty, I didn't believe he would do this. Hire someone to do it for him? Yes, of course. Once a ho dog, always a ho dog.

They all glanced at each other. The girls have an amazing way of communicating without moving any facial muscles or saying a word. The FBI should study them for their profilers' course. I had yet to figure it out.

"All indications are he's happy with wife number three," said Rhonda Jean, glancing around the table to see if there were any uneaten pizza slices left. "Sorry, Parker."

I just rolled my eyes and shook my head. "Who's doing it then? Surely, y'all must have some idea?"

Myrtle Sue looked up from licking her fingers. "Well, it's someone who doesn't much care for you, Parker. Everybody else's candy hearts have the standard "I love you" on them."

"Seriously, Myrtle Sue, you don't think I know that much?" I snapped. For as bright as these women could be on occasion, they could also be dumber than a box of Twinkies. Myrtle Sue had apparently picked up her box today.

"Who have you ticked off in the past week or so?" asked Misty Dawn with a slight twinkle in her eye.

"Aarrgghh!" I exploded. "No one. Denny's on vacation and should be back in a day or two. Missy is still handling everything in Atlanta and that's it! Well, there's Dewitt but he's too busy chasing after you to worry about me."

Denny is Denny Rowe, my head of security. He is a former black ops military guy and now heads up all things relating to my safety and well-being. He's about six feet tall, probably in the two-hundred-pound range, and has a hairy chest. Yes, I've seen it in a non-romantic way. While we bicker back and forth, there is absolutely no love chemistry between us. Other than the fact he's saved my life and is attractive in a military way, I could care less about him romantically.

Dewitt and Misty Dawn go to great lengths to antagonize each other. Even though Misty Dawn is in the Lady Gatorettes version of the witness protection program, she does like to taunt Dewitt whenever she's bored. She'll have someone call the sheriff's office and tell them Misty Dawn has been spotted speeding through town and that usually sets him off in hot pursuit. Meanwhile, she's sitting in a local business's parking lot eating a doughnut, drinking coffee, and laughing. It's all in a day's fun.

"Parker, the short version is we don't have a clue," Misty Dawn said.

My cell phone went off. Glancing at the caller ID, I scrunched up my mouth and my eyeballs headed north.

Everyone shouted, "Gracie Blanche!"

I nodded and answered. "Yes, Gracie Blanche?"

"Have you had any dealings with the mayor's office?"

I was perplexed. "Well, no, not really. I mean I had a meeting last week with the mayor, but it had to do with my cyber consulting company doing some work with the city. Why?"

"Because you've just been named for alienation of affection in a divorce between the mayor and his wife!" She giggled, "Have you engaged in adultery with the mayor?"

Yeah, like she had a lot of room to talk! She had had an affair with Scooter Travis, a city commissioner still married to his second or third wife. I forget which one it was. Unfortunately, he died. No, we're not going into reasons why or how he died.

ABOUT THE AUTHOR

O kay, true confession time. I have a wicked sense of humor, in case you hadn't noticed. My true desire and hope is that I made you laugh while reading this book.

Break the stress factor in your life for just a few minutes every day and do something that you enjoy doing that is just for yourself.

I absolutely love readers because without you I'd be eating peanut butter and crackers. Actually, I greatly appreciate you and your support. The best reward I get is when someone tells me they laughed out at my books and that it brightened their day.

People are always asking if I'm available for speaking engagements. The short answer is "Yes, of course." In fact, I can even do a Facebook Live Video event for your readers group.

Recommend it: Did you enjoy this book? Please let your friends, family, and even total strangers know about it!

Review it: Please tell other readers why you liked this book by reviewing it at Amazon or Goodreads. If you do write a review, please email me at Sharon@Sh aronEBuck.com so I can personally thank you. Remember, I appreciate you!

If you haven't read the first chapter of all the Parker Bell Cozy Mystery series, be sure to go to and download them.

Thank you for being a loyal fan!

ACKNOWLEDGMENTS

T hank you to my wonderful support team for your encouragement, words of reassurance, and belief in me on those days when the blank computer screen would stare back at me like a one-eyed monster daring me not to write anything. I survived and conquered.

Special thanks to Cindy Grooms Marvin, Marsha Davis-Flowers, Jennifer Bunderle, Pam Sheppard Minnick, Allegra Kitchens, Pat Ziegler, Wanda Strickland, Jodi Sykes, Jack Owen, Jordan Easton, Julie Zommers, and Barbara Smothers.

And, lastly, thank you to all my loyal readers and fans. I greatly appreciate you!

OTHER BOOKS BY SHARON E. BUCK

A Parker Bell Cozy Mystery

A Dose of Nice and Murder
A Honky Tonk Night and Murder